"You think I caused all this?"

"I think all of this is here because of your decision to fake your death. I think your arrogance has ruined many lives. Not only mine, but all these other people who care about you and are loyal to you."

He grimaced and shook his head. "I had to do it."

She was way too close to him. Close enough that she could smell his fresh, clean scent. She held her breath.

He ran his palm down her upper arm. "We need to talk. *I* need to talk, and you need to listen."

He held on to her for a few seconds, his head bent enough that he could look into her eyes. He wanted her to look at him. To yield to him.

She wouldn't. She couldn't. Not now. She had no idea what she was going to do, now that Rook was back. Yesterday he was dead. Today he was alive.

Until she could process everything that had happened in the past few hours, never mind the past two weeks or two years, she couldn't afford to allow herself to relax. She had to maintain control.

Control was all she had left.

MALLORY KANE

THE COLONEL'S WIDOW?

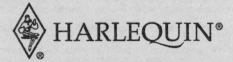

TORONTO • NEW YORK • LONDON
AMSTERDAM • PARIS • SYDNEY • HAMBURG
STOCKHOLM • ATHENS • TOKYO • MILAN • MADRID
PRAGUE • WARSAW • BUDAPEST • AUCKLAND

For Daddy, a hero by any definition.

Recycling programs
for this product may
not exist in your area.

ISBN-13: 978-0-373-69435-8

THE COLONEL'S WIDOW?

Copyright © 2009 by Rickey R. Mallory

www.eHarlequin.com

Printed in U.S.A.

ABOUT THE AUTHOR

Mallory Kane credits her love of books to her mother, a librarian, who taught her that books are a precious resource and should be treated with loving respect. Her father and grandfather were steeped in the Southern tradition of oral history, and could hold an audience spellbound for hours with their storytelling skills. Mallory aspires to be as good a storyteller as her father.

Mallory lives in Mississippi with her computer-genius husband, their two fascinating cats and, at current count, seven computers. She loves to hear from readers. You can write her at mallory@mallorykane.com or via Harlequin Books.

Books by Mallory Kane

HARLEQUIN INTRIGUE
927—COVERT MAKEOVER
965—SIX-GUN INVESTIGATION
992—JUROR NO. 7
1021—A FATHER'S SACRIFICE
1037—SILENT GUARDIAN
1069—THE HEART OF BRODY McQUADE
1086—SOLVING THE MYSTERIOUS STRANGER
1103—HIGH SCHOOL REUNION
1158—HIS BEST FRIEND'S BABY†
1162—THE SHARPSHOOTER'S SECRET SON†
1168—THE COLONEL'S WIDOW?†

†Black Hills Brotherhood

CAST OF CHARACTERS

Rook Castle—Two years ago, Rook faked his own death to keep his wife safe. But even that didn't stop terrorist Novus Ordo from targeting her. Now his cover has been blown, and Novus knows where he—and his wife—are.

Irina Castle—Her fight to find proof that her husband is alive has almost bankrupted Black Hills Search and Rescue and put her specialists in deadly danger. Now Novus is targeting her, and the only man who can save her is Rook. But he's supposed to be dead.

Deke Cunningham—Rook's best friend and part of the Black Hills Brotherhood.

Matt Parker—Matt risked everything to stand by the code of the Black Hills Brotherhood. He and the woman he loved became pawns in an international game of terror, with their lives and Rook's as the ultimate prize.

Aaron Gold—But is he the grateful son of an air force pilot who died a hero, or a bitter young man who blames Rook for his dad's death?

Brock O'Neill—This former navy SEAL can get the job done, but his private life is off-limits.

Rafiq Jackson—Does Rafe's quiet demeanor hide a sinister agenda?

Franklin Hill aka Frank James—He's brother to the international terrorist who kidnapped Deke's ex-wife to get to Deke.

Frederick Hill aka Novus Ordo—This faceless American expatriate wants to destroy America's dominance in the world. To do so he must remain anonymous; but one man, Rook Castle, can destroy him.

Chapter One

Moonlight sprinkled pale silver across Rook Castle's bare back, buttocks and thighs. His muscles tensed and rippled as he thrust once, twice, again and again, filling her with familiar, exquisite heat.

Irina's fingers slid through her husband's softly waving hair. She arched upward, pressing her breasts against his hot chest, demanding more.

He lifted himself, his biceps straining, glistening with sweat and moondust. He gave her more—gave her everything she craved. His deep, green stare mesmerized her.

"Rook," she whispered. "Why did you marry me?"

He went still. The moonlight no longer shimmered along his flanks and shoulders.

When would she learn to keep her mouth shut?

His arms quivered with effort as he held himself suspended above her. His arousal pulsed inside her.

"Rina—" he muttered, something between a warning and an endearment. Dipping his head, he sought her mouth.

She longed to kiss him, to surround herself with his powerful body, to feel him in her and around her as she had so many times before.

But her hands acted against her will and pushed at his chest. Resisting. She struggled to maintain eye contact. "Why?" she repeated.

"You know why," he whispered, his breath tickling her eyelashes.

"Tell me."

He kissed her eyelids, her cheek, the sweet spot below her earlobe. Then he moved, rocking her with a slow rhythm born of trust and familiarity. His chest rumbled with languid laughter when she gasped.

"Shh," he whispered. "Come with me."

She tasted sweat on his neck—salty, delicious. "Rook, please?"

With a frustrated sigh, he lifted his head. A jagged shadow defined his rigid jaw.

"I had to marry you," he said. "It was the only way I could protect you."

"But what about love?" Dear God, she was pathetic.

"Love? Rina, don't—" His voice rasped.

Then blood blossomed on his chest.

"No!" She reached for him, but her fingers slipped in the hot, sticky liquid.

"Rook!" she shrieked. "No! Help! Somebody help!"

He clutched at his chest.

She screamed.

His eyes met hers and he whispered something—she couldn't tell what.

She grabbed his arm, but he was too heavy. She couldn't hold on to him.

The last thing she saw was his beautiful face distorted by the bloodstained waters of the Mediterranean as he sank beneath its waves.

Irina Castle bolted upright, gasping for breath.

"No!" The word rasped past her constricted throat, pulling her out of the dream.

She wasn't on their yacht. She was at Castle Ranch, alone. She kicked the covers away and gulped in air. The taste of his sweat stung her tongue.

No. Not his sweat. Her tears.

Harsh moonlight glinted like a knife blade on every surface. She covered her face with her hands, trying to block it out.

She hated moonlight. Hated night. Darkness brought the fear, and moonlight brought the dream.

Every night she promised herself that next time she wouldn't ask him. Next time, she'd take all the dream would give and hold out for more. After all, her memories were all she had left.

But every night she asked.

Sliding out of bed, she reached to close the drapes and shut out the moon's light. But her skin burned and perspiration prickled the nape of her neck, so instead she flung open the French doors.

Cold air sent shivers crawling down her spine. She took another deep breath, hoping the sharp April chill would chase away the tattered remnants of her nightmare.

No such luck. Her body still quivered with unquenched desire. The empty place inside her still ached with grief.

In the distance, the Black Hills of Wyoming loomed in magnificent desolation. Rook had loved the mountains. He'd drawn strength and purpose from them. And like the Black Hills fed him, his strength, his dedication, his larger-than-life presence had fed her.

Then he'd been shot. His body was never recovered.

So for the past two years, she'd poured money into looking for him.

Two weeks ago, her accountant had issued an ultimatum—stop her unending search for Rook, or dissolve Black Hills Search and Rescue, the legacy he'd devoted his life to.

She stopped the search. How could she have known that her decision would set events in motion that would nearly destroy his two closest friends?

HE COULDN'T SLEEP. Hadn't been able to since he'd been released from the hospital. The idea that he'd been shot—*shot*—still spooked him. He was lucky to be alive.

So he sat up, looking out the window toward the ranch house. Toward Irina's bedroom. One of his favorite pastimes was watching her bedroom at night. She rarely closed the drapes.

He saw movement. Irina stepped out onto her patio with the red gown on—his favorite. She couldn't sleep, either. He watched her for a while, noticing that the pain from his gunshot wound wasn't so bad while he watched her.

Then he saw something—someone—inside the bedroom.

"Irina, don't tell me you've got a man in there," he whispered.

A cloud drifted by and the moonlight got brighter. He could see the man's face clearly. *Cunningham.* He'd know that hard face anywhere. What the hell was *he* doing in Irina's suite? At midnight?

He stood carefully, groaning with pain and dizziness, and got his shaving kit. Inside, hidden with the rest of his stash of goodies, was a LoJack.

It didn't matter what Cunningham was doing in

Irina's suite. What mattered was that he had a window of opportunity to keep up with his every move.

He sighed and clenched his teeth against the throbbing pain. He didn't want to go out there. He wanted to take another painkiller and go to bed. But he had a feeling this late-night meeting between Irina and Deke was no lovers' assignation.

From the way Irina was acting, she didn't know Cunningham was there.

Was this the night Cunningham would lead them to Rook Castle?

Pulling on a jacket, he stuck the LoJack in a pocket and took one more longing look at the bottle of painkillers on his bathroom sink. He needed one—bad. But he had to take care of business first.

Novus Ordo was willing to spend millions to find and capture his nemesis, Rook Castle.

He wanted at least one of those millions as a finder's fee.

BLACK HILLS SEARCH and Rescue specialist Deke Cunningham moved silently through the east wing of the sprawling ranch house. Behind him, beyond the enclosed courtyard, past the living room and kitchen, was the west wing, home of the offices of Black Hills Search and Rescue. The building to the south housed the staff quarters.

Hard to believe it had only been two weeks since Irina had called Matt Parker back from overseas.

A lot had happened, not the least of which was that he'd become a father.

Unbelievable. And thrilling. An involuntary grin stretched his mouth as he thought of Mindy and his newborn son.

On the heels of his grin came a wince. His tongue sought the cut on his lip that matched the one over his eye as he stopped in front of the door to Irina's suite.

Damn, he didn't want to be here. He wanted to be at the hospital with Mindy and their baby. He wanted to be planning their future together as a family.

But even more, he wanted to be in a different world. A world where his best friend hadn't had to die in order to save his wife. A world where a terrorist hadn't made it his mission to kill Rook Castle and everyone close to him.

But that world didn't exist. So he had to do his best to clean up this one—to make it safe for the people he loved. And one of those people was Irina Castle, Rook's widow.

He took a deep breath and glanced up and down the hall. There were four suites in the east wing. Irina's, of course. Next to hers was the one he'd lived in until he'd left on a mission to rescue his ex-wife, Mindy.

The suite directly across from his belonged to Rook's baby sister, Jennie. For the past two years, she'd been living in Texas with a family friend and attending graduate school. The fourth suite, opposite Irina's rooms, was empty.

Satisfied that there was no one around, Deke gripped the door handle. He'd waited until two o'clock in the morning for a reason. If he'd ever been on a stealth mission in his life, this was it.

The door was unlocked. "Dammit, Irina," he whispered. "You know the danger."

He eased open the door and peeked around it. Moonlight angled across the rumpled bed.

The rumpled, empty bed.

Instantly on alert, he drew his weapon as he slipped

inside and closed the door. A movement caught his eye. Curtains ruffling in the breeze. The French doors were open.

His unease ratcheted up a notch. Dan Taylor had assured him that there wasn't a chance in hell anyone could sneak past the Secret Service's perimeter onto the ranch. But Dan didn't know Novus Ordo.

Deke did.

He'd experienced firsthand what the internationally famous terrorist Novus was capable of. Twice. So it would take more than the word of a young hotshot with lots of civilian training and zero field experience to put him at ease.

Deke moved silently across the room, trying to position himself to see the entire patio without stepping out of the shadows. The French doors faced south, which meant she could be seen from the guesthouse, where the three specialists lived. If she was out there, they could see her—and him if he wasn't careful.

He knew from the gate guard that all three were there. And he had a very good reason for not wanting any of the three to know he was here.

He took another step, craning his neck to see the southwest corner. Finally, he saw a flash of red. There she was, in a red gown and robe, bathed in moonlight. She had her arms wrapped around herself, and her head was bowed.

He blew out his breath in relief and frustration. She was all right. But she was exposed. He sank back against the wall.

Now what?

He had to get her out of here and on the road. Every second increased the danger that he'd be spotted.

He thought about calling out to her, but if someone was watching, her reaction would alert them.

And once they were alerted, it wouldn't take them long to figure out that there was only one reason he'd be spiriting Irina away from Castle Ranch—the one place on earth she should be safe—in the middle of the night. And right now he couldn't risk anyone knowing where he was taking her. Not even his fellow BHSAR specialists.

Gritting his teeth, he waited, absently rubbing at the bandage on his right forearm. The surgeon had done a great job of stitching up his arm—thirty-two stitches—but the deep slash itched and hurt like a sonofabitch, courtesy of the weasel who'd called himself Frank James.

He'd like to have five minutes alone with James. Hell, three minutes would be plenty. But that was impossible. The dynamite he'd set off in a last-ditch effort to save Mindy and their unborn son had taken care of James and Novus Ordo's soldiers—permanently.

A rustle of silk pulled Deke's gaze to the French doors. Irina's shadow stretched across the bedroom floor. She was coming inside.

No matter what he did, his presence was going to scare her, so he stood still and waited until she stepped inside and closed the heavy drapes.

She headed toward the bed, reaching for the sash of the shimmery red robe. Then she stopped, her palm pressed against her midsection. She'd sensed him. Slowly, she turned her head.

"Irina," he said softly. "Stay quiet."

SHOCK PARALYZED Irina. She tried to suck in enough breath to scream, but her throat seized. She coughed and gasped.

"It's Deke," the voice said.

Deke. She shuddered as relief whooshed through her, followed by ringing alarm.

"Deke?" she said, her voice rising. "What's wrong?"

"Be quiet. Okay?"

She nodded.

"I'm serious. Promise?"

"Yes," she whispered. "Is it Mindy? Or the baby?"

He put two fingertips against her mouth. "They're fine. Listen. I've got to get you out of here."

Fear tore through her like lightning. It had happened. Danger had penetrated her home. She'd known it would one day.

"I'll get dressed," she whispered.

Deke shook his head and grabbed her hand. "No. No lights. No movement. I can't risk anyone knowing I was here."

Nothing Deke said made sense. "But—"

"Irina, we've got to go now."

IT DIDN'T TAKE Irina long to figure out where Deke was taking her. The route was familiar. They were headed to a hunting cabin Rook had acquired years ago. He'd managed to keep the title and tax papers in the name of the original owner and hadn't told anyone about it, except Deke and Matt, his oath brothers.

He'd called it their getaway house. A place the two of them could go where no one could find them if they didn't want to be found.

She hadn't been there since he'd died. Their last night there had been too painful to relive. Besides, why go alone?

Irina folded her arms beneath the wool throw Deke had tossed her way when he'd gotten into the SUV. She stared at the road, not bothering to hide her annoyance.

Several times, she'd tried to engage him in conversation, to no avail.

He acted as if he were too busy making sure they weren't being followed. Rook's best friend had always treated her with loving respect, but for whatever reason, tonight he wasn't answering any questions.

So she clamped her mouth shut and snuggled deeper under the throw. Her flimsy silk robe offered little protection against the late April chill. She shuddered. Nothing short of a direct and imminent threat would have made Deke ignore her comfort or dignity. Fortunately, she had clothes at the cabin.

Once they reached the hunting camp and Deke was satisfied that she was safe, she'd unload on him. She didn't get angry often—temper rarely helped any situation—but she didn't like being bullied. Not even by the man who'd appointed himself her protector after her husband's death, and not even if it was supposedly for her own good.

Deke spoke only once during the hour's drive, and then not even to her. He pulled out his cell phone and dialed a pre-programmed number. He listened for a few seconds.

"Dammit," he muttered. After another couple of seconds, he hung up and glanced at the tiny screen, as if to check the number he'd dialed. Then he shot her an awkward glance and turned his attention back to his driving.

Irina bit her tongue to stop herself from asking who he was trying to reach. He'd tell her when he felt like it.

The road ended a quarter mile from the camp, but Deke barely slowed down. He circled around and drove up behind the cabin, where he parked and shut off the engine of the large SUV.

Irina reached for the door handle.

"Wait," he snapped.

He retrieved his phone and pressed the redial button, hissing in frustration through clenched teeth.

After a few seconds, he sucked in a sharp breath. "Where have you been?" he growled.

Irina held her breath and listened, but she couldn't hear the person on the other end of the line.

"You could have waited. I was afraid you—" he stopped. "Yeah, okay. We're here. I'll bring her inside, then put the car in the barn." He paused, listening.

"Nope," he snapped. "No way. You're on your own this time. I'm going to take a look around. I'll be in later." He hung up and got out of the car.

Irina didn't bother to ask who'd been on the phone. Judging by the brevity of the conversation, she figured it was probably Brock, the oldest and most experienced of the Black Hills Search and Rescue specialists. Brock O'Neill's conversational style was terse at best.

As soon as she entered the rustic kitchen, she saw dim light coming from the front room. "Is that a fire? Or is the generator running?" she asked.

He didn't answer.

"Deke, stop acting like a secret agent and tell me what is going on! Who's here? Is it Brock?"

He set down his black duffel bag. "I'm not playing. Don't worry, you're safe. I'm going to hide the car. Irina—" He laid a hand on her arm, as if about to say something else.

She waited, apprehension crawling up her throat.

"Just remember that all this—was for you." He turned and went out the door, locking it behind him.

Irina stared at the door for a few seconds, as Deke's words replayed over and over in her head.

All this was for you.

"All of what?" she whispered. Shaking her head, she stepped through the dining room and into the front room. One lamp shone dimly, competing with the fireplace for the privilege of staving off the darkness. The only sound she heard was the crackling of the flames.

But she knew she wasn't alone.

Her breath hitched. Deke had promised her she was safe, she reminded herself. He'd promised her, ever since Rook's death, that he'd take care of her, and he had.

"Hello? Brock?" She spoke softly. "Is that you?"

No answer. Yet she felt a presence.

"Who's here?" she asked sharply.

Did she only imagine she heard breathing? She squinted, trying to see past the shadows. From the corner of her eye she recognized the old bookshelf to her right. It was on the wall opposite the fireplace. It was one of many places in the cabin where Rook had hidden loaded guns.

She'd never liked all the weapons. He'd turned their secret getaway into a secret arsenal. She'd complained a million times that she'd seen all the guns she ever wanted to see during her childhood in Russia. Still, she couldn't deny that right now she was glad to have a loaded weapon within reach. If she remembered correctly, this one was a Glock. She took a step toward the bookcase.

"Hello, Rina."

She whirled, startled. Nobody called her Rina—not anymore.

A lone figure stood to one side of the fireplace. All she could see was a silhouette.

"Who—?" Before she could gather breath to say

more, the person took a step forward. When the light hit his face, a giant fist grabbed her insides and wrung them tight—so tight she couldn't breathe.

"What's going on?" she gasped, gulping in air and casting about, as if an explanation lurked somewhere in the room.

"It's okay." A whisper. The figure held up a hand. "Irina…it's me."

A sharp ache burned through her chest. An ache of loss, of grief. Of denial.

"No," she breathed, shaking her head. Whoever was standing there, whatever was going on, she knew one thing for certain. His words were a lie. It wasn't him.

It couldn't be. He was dead.

She took a shuddering breath. "I—I don't understand—"

"I know you don't."

The sound of the man's voice sheared her breath and spasmed her throat. The words were tentative, the voice was hoarse and hesitant, but she knew it. Just like she knew the broad shoulders, the long powerful legs, the rugged profile outlined by the flickering firelight.

Knew them, yes. But believe what she heard and saw? No way.

It was impossible.

She clapped her hands over her mouth as her brain denied what her eyes saw. Was this another, more astounding dream? A dream she'd never—even in sleep—dared to contemplate?

Her hands slid down to cover her pounding heart. "Who are you?" she asked. "Where's Brock?"

He took another step forward.

She instinctively stepped backward, maintaining the distance between them. Her heartbeat thundered in her ears. Her throat closed up. Her whole body contracted, as if turning inward in an effort to protect her.

For an instant, her panicked brain considered running. Deke was in the barn. But she'd have to go past—

Her breath hitched.

His brows drew down and he took a step closer.

She stiffened, and he stopped.

She couldn't take her eyes off his face. His cheeks were leaner, his hair was all wrong—long and shaggy and damp, as if he'd just gotten out of a shower—and his eyes were haunted and sad. He was wearing dress pants without a belt, and a dress shirt that hung unbuttoned and untucked over the pants. And he was barefoot.

It was him.

Or a dream of him.

Darkness gathered at the edge of her vision, like a fade to black.

Like a dream. That had to be it. It was the only explanation that made sense.

She hadn't eaten dinner, and she'd drunk a glass of wine. Maybe she'd never woken up at all. She was still in bed, immersed in dreams. She pinched her arm, feeling silly.

Nothing changed.

The man standing in front of her lowered his gaze to the floor, then raised it again. When he did, a burning log collapsed, sending more light splashing across his face.

His face. The last time she'd seen those lean cheeks, that long straight nose, that wide sexy mouth, they had been horribly distorted by the dark Mediterranean waters.

"Go away," she cried. "Why are you doing this to me? You can't be here, Rook. You cannot. You are dead."

Chapter Two

God in Heaven, it was really her.

That was her low, sexy voice with the faint Russian accent that increased when she was upset.

Rook Castle wiped his palms down the legs of the dress pants that hung a bit too low on his haunches. His skin was still warm and damp from his shower, but the moisture on his palms came from pure nerves. He hadn't seen his wife in two years. Hadn't dared to hope he'd ever see her again.

She was so beautiful his eyes ached. More beautiful than he remembered. Although her delicate features were masked by fear, and her slender frame looked fragile, engulfed by the plaid wool blanket that wrapped around her shoulders.

Without makeup, her blue eyes surrounded by pale lashes were as wide and innocent as a girl's. And right now, they were filled with confusion and disbelief that etched another groove into his already battle-scarred heart.

"Irina," he breathed, and dared to move one step closer.

She held up a hand in warning. Her gaze tracked

him like a doe watching a hunter. He hated seeing her like that—the way she'd been when he'd rescued her father, dissident Soviet scientist Leonid Tankien.

But he'd come to know her well in the past six years. Irina Castle was no doe in headlights. In about five seconds that wild-eyed fear was going to change to fury, and woe to anyone who stepped into the path of her storm.

Woe to him.

"Irina." His throat was scratchy and sore, his voice hoarse from disuse. He'd talked more today than he had in two years. He cleared his throat. "I'm not—"

"What is going on?" She stiffened her back and tucked her chin. Her eyes narrowed and the spark he'd been waiting for flashed in them. She eased sideways. Again.

A weak thrill fluttered in his chest. If he could've remembered what muscles to use to smile, he would have.

She was doing exactly what he'd expected her to do. She was edging toward the closest weapon—a Glock .23, hidden in a shelf of dog-eared paperbacks opposite the fireplace.

He pushed back his open shirt and slid his weapon from the paddle holster in his waistband. He held it up. "Here," he said, flipping the Sig Sauer's handle out. "Take mine."

He bent down and slid it across the red oak floor toward her, then straightened and leaned against the mantel, doing his damnedest to appear nonchalant.

She picked up the gun, never taking her eyes off him. The blanket slipped off her shoulders, and Rook saw her perfectly shaped breasts beneath a thin covering of silk. He gritted his teeth as his body reacted to the familiar, lush curves and hollows he saw, and those he knew only from memory. Her beautiful body, which he'd yearned for every night during the past two years.

Was that the red silk gown and robe she'd bought for their yachting cruise in the Mediterranean? He'd never gotten to see it on her.

He'd died on that trip. As the thought formed in his head, the heat in his groin dissipated.

Clutching the Sig, Irina pointed it at him and straightened. One shoulder of the robe slid down her arm. She didn't notice.

Her delicate shoulder was made more vulnerable, more fragile looking by the little bump of bone that interrupted its curve. Her skin stretched across it, appearing translucent. He knew that bump, and the matching one on the other side. He knew how it felt, how it tasted. Like clean, white linen. Like her.

Rook winced inwardly and lifted his gaze to her face. Her gaze met his with faint horror, as if he were a stranger ogling her and she could read his thoughts.

Suddenly, a different kind of sparkle lit her eyes, and it twisted his heart painfully.

He knew better than anyone that Irina never cried. And he knew why. That he'd caused the tears that reflected the firelight gouged another chunk from his heart.

She took a deep breath, lifted her chin and, miraculously, the dampness in her eyes disappeared.

"So tell me. What is the big emergency?" she asked tonelessly.

"What?"

"Obviously, you never planned to—" she paused briefly "—to come back here. But something has happened. Something involving me. Something you couldn't handle any other way."

She wrapped her left hand around her right to support the weight of the gun. "You were never fond of theatrics, so I have to assume that it is urgent, or you wouldn't have sneaked me out here in the dead of night. So get to it."

Rook nodded. *That's my girl.*

She was doing everything she could to stay in control. It was one of the things he loved about her. That need to keep everything steady in an unsteady world. It was embedded into the core of steel that had drawn him to her the first time he'd seen her. But that steel core made her slow to trust.

And if anyone ever betrayed her…

If he could hate himself any more than he already did, he would. But his self-loathing was maxed out. There was no way he could explain to her why he'd done what he had.

Hell, *he'd* been second-guessing his decision for two years.

"Is it because of what happened to Matt and Deke? I'm sure Deke has briefed you—" Her voice cracked.

"Deke didn't know," he said quickly. "Not for sure. Not until yesterday morning. Don't blame him."

"No. I do not blame him. I blame you." The staccato words were coated with frost. "Spare me the explanations. Just get to the point."

"Why don't you sit down—"

"Get. To. The. Point!"

Rook pushed his hands through his hair and wiped his face. He still wasn't used to his naked cheeks and chin. The beard—his mask—had been a part of him for the past two years. He lifted his gaze to Irina's. Her eyes were as hard and opaque as turquoise.

"Novus Ordo is after you."

"Da," she said, then, "Yes. That I know."

"When you stopped looking for me, and called Matt back to Wyoming, it alerted him. Deke was right about—"

"About Novus acting on the theory that I stopped because I had found you," she fired back at him in a rapid staccato. "Not because I ran out of money or gave up. How silly of me. I waste so much time and money looking for you when I could have—" her voice broke and she laughed sharply, the sound like breaking glass. "You should tell me something I do not know."

"Fine. But I'm going to sit down. You stand there if you want." Rook dropped into a worn leather chair that smelled like oil and pipe smoke. It had been his dad's.

He couldn't believe how shaky he was. How unsure. He didn't remember ever feeling this way before. Back when he'd made the decision to fake his death to stop Novus Ordo from targeting Irina, he'd felt like his life was spiraling out of control.

But *this* uncertainty was new—born of lies and deception, of stealth and secrecy and living in exile.

He'd been alone too long. In the past two years he'd barely spoken a word to another person. He'd spent all his time studying and searching for his enemy. The world's most dangerous terrorist, Novus Ordo.

He feared he might never feel human again, now that he'd lived inside himself for so long. He'd hoped to find a way to keep up with her, to make sure she was all right.

But by the time he was healed, he knew if he saw her he wouldn't be able to stay away from her.

And if he didn't stay away from her, she could die.

When he looked up, she hadn't moved, although the gun barrel had tilted downward. Her face was still expressionless, but her body was rigid—so tense he was afraid her bones might break.

"You said you know Novus Ordo is after you. Do you understand why?"

Irina's throat moved as she swallowed. "I understand that it has to do with you. That secret mission to save the senator's son, before you left the Air Force." She took a shaky breath. "When you rescued Deke." Then she shot him a look of pure suspicion. "Not that *you* ever told me anything about it."

"Do you know why Novus wants me?"

She shrugged and her arms dropped. The Sig slid from her fingers and hit the floor with a thud. "You saw him."

He nodded wearily. "Apparently I'm the only person in two hemispheres, other than his trusted inner circle, who's ever seen him without his mask."

"Why didn't you kill him then, when you had the chance?"

He shrugged without lifting his head. "We've been through this. I was out of ammo. I was sure I was a dead man."

Irina moaned audibly. "But now, you're not the only one who knows what he looks like. The CIA has the drawing. Why can't they figure out who he is? Find him? Kill him?"

"Believe me, Irina, if it were that simple—"

"No!" She shook her head, and the clip that had been holding her hair slipped free and clattered to the floor. Waves of shimmering gold fell over her shoulders.

He swallowed against the lump that suddenly rose in his throat.

"No," she repeated. "Believing you is something I will never do again."

Rook slammed his fist down on the arm of his leather chair. "Then what do you want from me?" he yelled.

Too late, he realized he'd done what he always did when backed into a corner. He'd turned a weak defense into a strong offense.

And this time he'd aimed it at his wife. *His wife.* The one person in the world who least deserved it. Who had never deserved what loving him had put her through.

She winced, then lifted her chin. "I want the truth. But, as I am sure you can understand, I'm a little shy right now."

Gun-shy, he almost said, but he bit his tongue. She'd always laughed when he'd correct her English. She wouldn't appreciate it now.

"Why don't you ask the questions, and I'll answer them."

"Truthfully?"

Rook growled and rubbed his aching jaw. The muscles there and in his neck throbbed with tension.

"Did you plan all this?" she snapped.

He looked up at her from beneath his brows. "All what?"

Irina let fly a string of Russian that Rook was sure would have shocked her father, were he still alive.

"Sorry," he muttered, feeling mean and cornered and exposed. "I planned to die. It was the only choice I had—"

He clenched his jaw and pressed his lips together. No. She didn't deserve excuses.

He propped his forearms on his knees and nodded, looking down at the floor.

"If you planned the whole thing, then who did you hire to shoot you?"

He bent his head and squeezed his temples between his palms. He was tired. He was frustrated. He ached with the need to pull her into his arms. Just long enough to remind himself that he was a human being. That he was alive.

He hadn't felt anything in so long, he'd begun to wonder if he ever would.

"Rook? Who shot you?"

Her voice sizzled with venom. She hated him for what he'd done to her. And she had every right.

His very presence here put her in danger—her and everyone else involved with Black Hills Search and Rescue. That thought sent a shard of fear through his chest.

No. He couldn't afford to feel anything—not until all this was over. If he let his emotions get in the way, the consequences would be too great to bear.

He'd already pushed Irina too far. Answering the question she'd asked would sever the last frayed thread that bound them together. And he wasn't sure he could survive if that thread broke.

He took a long breath. "Deke."

Irina gasped audibly. "What?"

He lifted his head and met her shocked gaze. "You heard me," he muttered.

"D-deke?" she stammered.

As she spoke, the door from the kitchen opened.

"Deke shot you?" Her voice was shrill with shock.

"Oh, crap," Deke said.

IRINA MET the wary gaze of her husband's best friend. She shook her head back and forth—back and forth, while her stomach churned with nausea.

"I don't understand…" she whispered. Her throat was too tight, her chest too constricted, to speak any louder.

"Don't blame him," Rook said, standing.

He might as well have been in a different room. She barely heard him. All she could do was stare at Deke, who had been there for her, who had grieved with her, who had kept Black Hills Search and Rescue going and had taken care of her during the dark time since her husband's death.

"Deke? You—?"

"Irina, he was only following—" Rook started.

"Shut up!" She swiped a hand through the air in his general direction without looking at him.

Deke's tanned faced turned a sickly green. He opened his mouth, closed it, ducked his head and rubbed the back of his neck. "Irina—"

"You shot him? You shot Rook? It was you?" Saying it didn't make it any more real. In fact, it confused her more. The memory of those awful seconds washed over her like a volcanic wind. For that instant she was back there, on the deck of their yacht, feeling the downdraft from the helicopter, gripping Rook's arm as she asked him why it was flying so close.

"But that's impossible. The shot—it came from a helicopter. He was—" She turned her head to look at Rook. "You were hit in the chest. All that blood…" She had to force air past her constricted throat.

"It was so awful. How could you not tell me, Deke?"

"It was…a matter of national security—" Deke started.

"He was following my orders. He didn't know I was still alive until he contacted a prearranged number three days ago."

Irina's head was spinning. Too much information. "But I saw the bullet hit you. It made a little puff." She gestured with her fingers. "F-fibers from your shirt, I think. Then blood—your blood—spattered on my blouse. You fell into the water." She pressed her palms to her temples. "Were you wearing a bulletproof vest? No, you couldn't have been. We'd just…" Her voice trailed off as more memories flashed across her vision.

They'd made love. She'd watched him dress afterward. All at once she realized that was the origin of her recurring dream.

They'd made love and then he'd been shot.

Killed.

"I watched you die," she whispered. Then suddenly the floor tilted and her vision turned dark. Strong arms enveloped her.

Rook's arms. But no. It couldn't be. Rook was dead.

She came awake as he laid her gently on the sofa. She didn't open her eyes, afraid the room would tilt again. Afraid her world would turn right-side up again and Rook would be gone.

The next thing she was aware of was Deke's voice.

"—can't believe you're here in the flesh. But I gotta say, I'd like to strangle you right now. You could have let me know you were alive."

"After all that planning, it was too risky to take a chance like that. What happened to your arm?"

Their words confirmed what Rook had said. The two men, who'd been best friends and oath brothers since childhood, really hadn't spoken in two years. She could tell from Deke's voice that he'd feared he'd killed his best friend.

At least Deke hadn't betrayed her—not like her husband had.

"This? It's just a scratch, courtesy of a costume cowboy called Frank James, who insisted he wasn't working for Novus."

"It's wrapped up like a mummy. Looks like a little more than a scratch."

"Don't worry about me. I'm fine. More than I can say for your *widow*. Think she's okay?"

"I think so. But look at her. She's so pale, so scared. Dear God, I never meant to hurt her."

"Well, you did."

"You think I don't know that? If there had been any other way—"

"You know what, man? Just stop. I had to watch her, knowing the whole time what I'd done—what I'd let you do. I've learned a lot in the past two years. And even more in the past few days. One thing I can tell you for sure, it may take me the rest of my natural life to make up to Mindy for everything I put her through in the past. But I'll do it. And I won't waste time whining that there was nothing else I could do." Deke's voice was low, but Irina heard the disgust and anger behind his words.

Cloth squeaked against leather as Rook stood up. "You got anything else to say, Cunningham? Because if you do, maybe we should go outside. I'd rather my wife not be any more upset than she already is."

"Now you're blaming me for upsetting her? You arrogant—"

Their argument was fast escalating into a fight. Irina sat up, a lot more quickly than she should have. Stars flared at the edge of her vision. She pushed her hair out of her face.

Both men turned toward her. She could see Deke's sheepish expression and Rook's worried gaze through the fading starbursts.

"Hey, Irina." Deke's voice softened into gentleness. "Are you okay?"

"Not even near," she muttered.

"Stay still. Rest. Maybe you can even sleep for a while," Rook said.

She laughed. "Sleep? I don't know what sleep is. Not for two years. My brain is speeding ninety miles an hour. There are so many questions that I don't know where to start."

His gaze faltered.

"Okay. Answer this one. Why did Deke bring me here?"

Deke answered her. "Because he doesn't want you out of our sight for even one second."

She shook her head and smiled sadly. "No. That doesn't explain it. Why now? I've been out of your sight for two years—" She stopped. "Or have I? Don't tell me you have watched me all this time." Her stomach churned. "I think I may be sick."

"I swear, this is the first time I've set foot in the U.S. I couldn't chance being spotted."

She turned to Deke. "So how did you find him?"

Deke's gaze slid past her to Rook. "I'll let you field that one. I'm going to go take a look around outside—"

"No!"

Deke and Rook jumped.

She swallowed. Her vehemence surprised even herself. "No. You stay right here, Deke. You're involved in this, too."

Deke looked down at the toe of his boot.

Rook rubbed a hand across his face. Despite her hurt and anger, Irina's heart squeezed at the soul-deep weariness etched there.

"I set up a message service," he said flatly. "The fees are paid automatically on a yearly basis by electronic withdrawal from a bank in the Caymans. I used the name Kenneth Raven."

She stared at him. "A bank—" How had she been married to him and not known him at all?

"So who called you on this message service? I thought Deke did not know you were alive. You said nobody knew."

"That's right. Nobody. Deke had the number, but he wasn't to call it unless it was a life-or-death situation."

"You arranged your assassination. You planned for a contingency in case you needed—or wanted—to return to life. You left your sister, your wife, all your friends and family, to think you were dead." Irina's stomach was still churning. Her head was spinning. "We had a funeral. We grieved for you. And the whole time you were laughing at us."

"Trust me, I wasn't laughing."

Was she seeing things, or were his eyes brighter than they'd been a few seconds ago? She'd never seen Rook Castle cry before. Still, even if those were tears, it didn't matter. It was too late for tears, too late for apologies.

It was too late.

An awful thought occurred to her. "What about Jennie? Is she all right?"

He nodded without looking at her. "I hired a bodyguard for Jennie, using the Cayman Islands account. She has no idea."

"So you have decided the best thing for everybody, haven't you?"

"I didn't have a choice."

She lifted her chin. "Just so I know, how long had you been planning all this?"

"Rina, it wasn't like that—"

"How…long?"

Out of the corner of her eye she saw Deke squeeze his eyes closed.

Rook looked away and shrugged. "Six months. Maybe eight."

A short, sharp laugh burst from her throat. "Eight *months*. You lived with me, you made love to me, and all the time you were planning to—? Dear God, who are you?"

She stood and caught the arm of the sofa to steady herself. Then she glared at the man she'd married in a fever six years ago. "I do not know you at all."

Rook spread his hands. "Trust me, it'll all make more sense once you've had some rest. It's a lot for you to take in right now—"

"A lot to take in? You think?" She heard her voice rising in pitch. "But, yes, of course. I am sure I'll feel much better once I take a *nap*."

Deke reached out a hand, as if to soothe her, but she jerked away. "No. Don't touch me."

She wrapped her arms around her middle and turned back to Rook. "Where have you been? Who have you been in touch with?"

"Nobody. Irina, you need to calm down."

"You have no right to tell me what I need to do. You gave that up when you let me think you were dead." She held up her hands, palms out. "I can't—I cannot take any more. I'm going to make tea."

"Stay there. I'll make it for you," Deke said.

"No," she snapped. She couldn't be alone with Rook. She didn't know what she would do—or say. "I think I'll let you two talk. It's pretty obvious you need to."

She glared at Deke. "Maybe you can get some real answers out of him."

She took a cautious step, making sure her legs weren't going to collapse, then headed to the kitchen, with Rook's voice following her.

"Use the light over the stove. Don't turn on the overheads."

"Fine. Fine. No problem," she muttered. "Like I have no sense to figure that out."

She twisted her hair up and anchored it with a rubber band from a kitchen drawer, then pulled the tea canister toward her, hoping there was at least one tea bag. She opened the lid.

"Jasmine," she whispered. Her favorite. She dug the little package out and opened it.

She put the kettle on the stove eye and held the tea bag to her nose. The scent hurtled her back in time.

She and Rook had come up here a couple of weeks before the fateful trip to the Mediterranean. Just the two of them.

She'd brought up the idea of having a baby— again. And again, like always, he'd sidetracked her with jasmine tea and hot, passionate lovemaking. He'd never talked about having children. At least now she understood why.

She had to blink away tears before she could pour the hot water into her mug. Then she turned out the light over the stove and stood at the kitchen window in the dark, waiting for the tea to steep. In the distance, thunder rolled lazily and a pale flash of lightning lit the sky.

Before Rook, she'd always been afraid of thunderstorms. They reminded her of the guns and bombs from her childhood in the former Soviet Union. Thunderstorms had frightened her. But ever since she'd married Rook, she'd learned to love them.

He liked to lie in bed with the windows open, summer or winter, spring shower or gale-force winds, and watch the lightning and listen to the sounds of rain and thunder. For her, lying in his arms, safe and secure in the knowledge that he would never let anything happen to her, was the ultimate definition of safety.

But he'd left her alone—alone with the storms and the memories and the unrelenting grief.

She swiped her fingers under her eyes and set the tea bag aside. Then she wrapped her hands around the warm mug and sipped, sighing as the hot liquid slid down her throat to soothe her insides.

She closed her eyes. She'd spent the past two years living in a nightmare. Every night, she'd prayed she would wake up and find Rook beside her, safe and sound. Every morning, she'd woken with her prayer unanswered.

Now he was here, but she still didn't feel like her prayers had been answered.

This felt like the nightmare. The months of sleepless nights, of the recurring dream of loving him and then losing him, had become her reality.

Thunder rumbled again, closer this time. Irina's eyes flew open. A lightning flash illuminated the dense woods on the east side of the cabin and a deafening clap of thunder made her nearly spill her tea.

Then something moved—a shadow darker than the trees.

She froze, holding her breath as the thunder continued to roar. She waited for the next flash of lightning. It didn't take long.

The flare spotlighted a creature slinking along the edge of the woods. No. Not a creature. Not some *thing*.

Someone. And he was carrying a gun.

Chapter Three

Irina's breath caught. There was someone outside the cabin, and he was carrying a weapon—maybe a rifle.

Setting down her mug, she moved swiftly toward the living room.

Rook and Deke were still arguing.

"—surprised he hasn't tried to get to Rina before now," Rook was saying.

"Son of a— That's what I'm trying to tell you. He has." Deke's voice rose. "You don't get it. The level of security I've got around her—she might as well be the First Lady. I told you I'd take care of her!"

"Of course I get it. That's not what I'm saying."

"It's only been two weeks since she called off the search. Fifteen days! And he's already managed to send a man after Matt and put a plan into place to kidnap Mindy. That's why I knew I had to call you. He was obviously watching Matt. He knew the instant Irina called him. Hell, he knew before she got in touch with Matt. I'm thinking Novus knew she was calling off the search as soon as we did."

"That's not possible," Rook snapped.

"It is if he's got a mole on the inside. Look how he

got to Mindy and used her to get to me. The SOB was watching her. He knew she was pregnant, something neither Irina nor I knew."

"You can't think that one of the BHSAR specialists is working for Novus."

Irina stepped into the room.

"Would you listen?" Deke snapped. "My helicopter was sabotaged on the ranch. Right there in front of the hangar."

"Sabotaged?"

"Rook! Deke!" Irina hissed. "There is someone outside. He's armed."

"What?" Both men jumped up. Deke grabbed a fireplace tool and shoveled ash over the flames. "Where?"

"At the edge of the woods outside the kitchen window."

"Did he see you?" Rook asked.

She shook her head. "Not when I saw him. The lights were off. Maybe while I was making the tea."

"I thought you said you weren't followed," Rook flung at Deke.

"I wasn't. You?"

"Absolutely not. Are they Secret Service?"

"I've got a team on alert, but they won't approach until I call them." Deke cursed. "See? This is what I've been trying to tell you—"

"Who'd you tell about the cabin?"

"Just Dan Taylor. Today."

"Then how in hell did they find us? LoJack?"

"No way. I swept the SUV before I picked up Irina."

"But not after? If what you said about a traitor in BHSAR is true, someone could have tapped your car while you were inside."

Deke cursed and crossed the room. He peered through the corner of the wooden blinds.

Rook shook his head. "No matter. Too late now. Are there still automatic weapons in the safe?" he asked as he walked over to the metal safe set into the far wall.

"Yeah, plenty. I can't see anything out there."

Rook dialed in the code and opened the heavy door. He reached in and pulled out two machine guns, along with several magazines of ammunition. "Wow," he breathed. "You've upgraded."

Deke walked back over to the fireplace. "HK 416s," Deke said. "Secret Service gave me those after you disappeared. Part of their commitment to protecting Irina. You should find some super-hot night-vision goggles in there, too. And several flash grenades."

"Nice." Rook examined one of the 416s briefly and efficiently. His ease with handling the big weapon sent chills down Irina's spine.

Deke pulled out his phone and dialed a number. He spoke a few words and hung up. "The Secret Service team will be here in less than twenty."

"Hand me a com unit. And don't we have some Tasers around here?"

Deke had already pulled a small wired box out of his pocket. "Pocket Tasers and handcuffs are stowed in the duffel bag I brought in."

Irina watched them in awe. They hadn't seen or talked to each other in two years, yet they worked completely in synch, anticipating each other's needs. Their calm efficiency was reassuring and yet profoundly frightening at the same time.

As he grabbed the com unit and inserted the earpiece, Rook nodded at Irina. "You're going to the basement."

"Wait. I can take the Sig. I can help——"

"Now!" He pointed a finger at her. "And don't open the door until you hear my signal. There's a Glock down there, with plenty of extra ammo. Remember the safe word?"

She nodded stiffly, nearly paralyzed with fear. Years ago, when Rook had bought the cabin, he'd extended the basement to the barn and turned it into a safe room, reinforced with steel.

Since the barn was downhill from the cabin, a short tunnel was all that was necessary to join the two buildings. A door at the far end of the basement joined the back wall of the barn.

He'd gone over a long list of precautions with her. His insistence on such extensive safety measures had spooked her at the time, but they'd never had to use any of them.

For her, Rook's very presence had always meant safety. But no more. The man standing in front of her with cold determination hardening his face was not the same man she'd married.

"Go!" he barked.

"Don't—" she choked out through her constricted throat "—don't get killed."

ROOK DECIDED to follow Irina down the stairs from the pantry to the basement. He wasn't going to take any chances. He'd see for himself that she was securely locked in the basement safe room.

He didn't touch her—he didn't have to, to know that she was shivering with fear and confusion. That and more radiated from her like a fever. He couldn't blame her, but he couldn't reassure her, either.

He wanted to tell her how sorry he was. Wanted to somehow explain. But even if he could form the words, they were meaningless. Mere words couldn't make up for what she'd been through.

Hell, nothing could.

He opened the basement door and stepped back to let her pass. She went through the reinforced metal door and pushed it almost closed, then paused, peering at him through the narrow opening.

Long ago, he'd promised her that she would never be afraid again. He'd promised himself that she'd never have cause to regret marrying him. He'd broken both promises.

"Why?" she whispered, as if she knew his thoughts. "Why did you let me believe you were dead? All this time—"

He clenched his jaw. "Not now, Rina."

She recoiled slightly, as if dodging a blow.

He'd hurt her again. More. It seemed that all he'd ever be able to do from now on was hurt her.

Reassuring words lodged in his throat. If he said them, they could turn into yet another lie. She needed time to heal, time to learn that she could trust him.

But right now time was a luxury they couldn't afford, because Novus had found them. So he said nothing.

She lowered her gaze and closed the door.

Rook stood there until he heard the massive lock click into place, then he mounted the stairs.

He tapped the ultralight communications transmitter in his ear.

"Deke?" he muttered.

"Front room. And whisper, dammit. You're busting my eardrums." Deke's words slid through his head as if they were his own thoughts.

"Irina's secure," he mouthed, barely making a sound. "I'm in the kitchen. Whatcha got?"

"I see two, slinking around behind the trees."

Deke's voice was clear and as smooth as silk. These were damn good units. A far cry from the staticky ones they'd used during their Air Force missions.

"I figure there are four of them," Deke continued. "And two of us. That makes it even odds."

Rook's mouth twitched. "You're giving those four guys a lot of credit."

"Yeah, well, they may have explosives. How do you want to handle this?"

"The two you don't see—where are they?"

"My guess—one at the front door and one at the back, waiting for us to come out. I'm betting Novus wants you alive, so they'll try tear gas first. Then escalate to stun grenades if they have to."

"What about these grenades we've got?"

"New toy, courtesy of Homeland Security. Works like a regular grenade. The flash blinds the enemy for thirty seconds or so. The goggles you've got hanging around your neck will protect you."

"What if they have the goggles, too?"

"These babies are brand-new technology. Prototypes. Theory is you can stare at the sun for hours with them on. I doubt Novus has them yet. *We* don't have them—officially. Whoa!"

"What?"

"They're on the move."

"Deke, go get Rina and get the hell out of here. Through the basement into the barn. The keys are in the rental car. I'll hold them off."

"The hell you will! Four against one's not the same as four against two. You'll be playing right into their hands. You get Irina, I'll hold off these—" Deke spilled a few choice curse words. "I've gotten away from Novus twice before. I can do it again."

"With that arm you may not be able to handle the 416. It's heavy."

"You don't worry about me. I can handle anything you can."

Rook heard something clatter against the kitchen window. "Something hit the window. Probably tear gas."

"Rook—go! Take Irina and get to safety. They're after you, not me."

"No way. We'll take them together and then I'll get Rina. As long as she stays in the safe room, she'll be fine."

"Unless one of our visitors decides to check out the barn."

"The steel door from the barn into the safe room is rated for twenty minutes against dynamite."

"Good to know. So how do we want to take these guys? Stay together or split up?"

"You take the front. I'll take the back and then we'll catch the middle two in a crossfire. No casualties unless absolutely necessary. I want them in custody, spilling their guts."

He heard a hissing noise outside the window. "There goes the tear gas. They wasted that one."

"I'm at the door. You?"

Rook flattened his back against the kitchen door, mentally measuring the distance out to the yard. The door opened onto a small stoop and then down five steps. "Yeah. See anything?"

"Nah. I say we go on three. If you spot one, try the flash grenade, but be ready with firepower. I'll be shooting down from the porch." The edge in Deke's voice cut like a razor blade through Rook's head. He knew the tone. Deke was prepared to die to protect him. Rook felt the same way.

But it wasn't going to happen. Not today—not ever. Deke had every reason to stay alive. He had Mindy and their newborn baby boy.

And Rook had— He gripped his machine pistol in both hands and shoved those thoughts away. "On my mark," he growled.

"One." He tensed his thighs and pushed to a standing position, then pulled the night-vision goggles over his eyes. It took him a second to adjust to the *Matrix*-like look of the world through the infrared lenses.

"Two." He turned the key in the back door and reached for the knob, ready to angle around. Ready for anything. A heady rush of adrenaline buzzed through him, making him super-aware. He heard the whisper-light hum of a mosquito, noticed the faint cold breeze on his neck.

He took a long, slow breath.

"Three!" He slung the door open and slid around it, his finger on the trigger of the HK 416. The 416 was a heavy piece of equipment and carried plenty of ammo, but right now its weight was comforting.

A second wave of adrenaline jacked up his heart rate and sharpened his already-honed senses.

Deke's labored breathing sounded like a windstorm above the sawing of his own breaths. His nose picked up the fresh, earthy smell of rain from the brief thunderstorm. His trigger finger tightened.

In one long stride, he crossed the stoop and put his back against a wooden pillar.

Poised to shoot, he swung out and swept the backyard with his gaze and his gun. It was empty—no shadowy figures, no sound other than rain dripping off eaves and tree branches.

Where were they? If they were his men, they'd be covering the main entrances to the cabin.

He didn't like that he couldn't see them. Had they circled around to the barn? Or was Deke wrong? Were there just two of them?

He shook his head. Deke was rarely wrong.

"Whatcha got?" he whispered into the com mic.

"Nothing." Deke's voice was laced with disgust.

"Still think there are four of them?"

"Yeah. But maybe not."

A noise to Rook's left had him swinging his weapon in that direction. Glass shattered.

"They breached the kitchen window with a tear-gas grenade. Ready to go? Flash grenade first?"

"On your mark," his friend replied.

"One…" Rook hopped lightly to the ground and planted his back against the north wall of the cabin, east of the porch. The grass, wet from the thunderstorm, muffled his footsteps.

"Two…" He cradled the HK 416 in his right arm and pulled out a flash grenade with his left, noticing his arm, dark and edged with acid green, through the goggles.

"Three!"

He rounded the corner of the cabin in time to see a human-shaped green monster slink away from the kitchen window back toward the woods.

He jerked the pin with his teeth and tossed it a couple of feet beyond the man.

"Flash!" he muttered into his com unit. "Look out."

Suddenly the yard lit up like the midway of a state fair. Even through the goggles the flare was painfully bright. Someone screeched in pain.

Then all hell broke loose.

The air around him filled with the deep rat-tat-tat of

machine-gun fire. The blinded enemy were strafing the yard randomly, hoping to score a hit.

And coming damn close.

Rook shrank against the wall, making himself as small as possible as a flurry of bullets zinged past him. If he could dodge them long enough, their attackers would soon be out of ammo.

If he could dodge them.

"Deke?"

"I'm okay. You?"

"Soon as they're done wasting ammo, let's take them. Tasers and cuffs. Then we'll see how many buddies they've got."

"Say the word."

Rook stayed flattened against the wall until he heard the spit of machine-gun fire slow down and then stop. The volley that seemed to go on forever had probably only lasted a few seconds.

He pulled the fully charged Taser from the scabbard he'd attached to his belt and checked its setting.

Medium. He turned it to high. To the danger zone, in fact. He wanted the bastards helpless and moaning with muscle cramps.

Then, with his finger on the trigger of the HK 416, he tensed.

"Go!" he spat through the com unit.

He rounded the northeast corner of the house just as Deke appeared on the southeast end of the long front porch.

The guy who'd thrown the tear gas was dressed head to toe in black. He lurched across the bare yard toward the woods, obviously still blinded by the high-powered flash. Rook hoped Deke had the other man in his sights.

He slung the 416 over his shoulder by its strap and

ran toward the stumbling terrorist. He took him down easily, zapped him with the Taser and then, ignoring his moans, cuffed him and jerked his ski cap over his eyes as a blindfold.

"Move, and I'll shock you again."

The man squealed in protest. His legs jerked involuntarily.

The unmistakable stacatto of machine-gun fire broke the silence.

"Deke?"

"Over here. I got two for one. Had to take one out. Got the other one trussed up like a turkey."

"Mine, too. That makes three."

"Hey." Deke's voice brightened. "Here comes the cavalry, right on time."

As his voice faded, Rook saw the headlights. He jerked his captive to his feet by the neck of his black sweater, but the man's legs buckled under him.

"Get moving. I'll drag you if I have to," Rook growled and proceeded to do just that. By the time he got to Deke his arm muscles were protesting.

Rook dumped the man onto the ground next to Deke's prisoner and shoved his goggles up onto his forehead. "Where's the casualty?"

Deke nodded toward the bushes that hugged the edge of the porch. At that moment, the headlights of a black SUV shone on them like spotlights, and four Secret Service agents jumped out, dressed in flak jackets with weapons at the ready. The driver stepped over next to Deke while the other two took charge of the prisoners.

"Good timing, Dan," Deke said, nodding at the driver.

Rook glanced beyond the SUV as a second vehicle pulled up and four more flak-jacketed men emerged.

"Rook, meet Special Agent Dan Taylor, with the

Secret Service. He just took over as Agent in Charge of Security around the ranch. He's been briefed about your situation. Dan, this is Colonel Rook Castle."

Taylor shook his hand. "Pleasure, Colonel."

"Glad to meet you," he said. "Deke, I'm going to get Rina."

Deke nodded as he continued talking with Taylor. "Dan, we think these guys are working for Novus Ordo. I'm afraid the one in the bushes over there didn't make it, but these two are healthy. We need all the intel they've got."

"Any means necessary?" the Secret Service agent asked.

"That's right," Deke responded. It looked to Rook like Deke had everything handled for the moment. So he turned on his heel and headed for the house to fetch Irina from the fortified basement.

As soon as Deke and Agent Taylor headed off with the prisoners, and he and Irina were finally alone, they could talk. The thought sent apprehension skittering down his spine.

He was halfway up the steps to the kitchen door when the blast shook the cabin. The force of the explosion knocked him down the steps and on his butt. Heated air gushed over him.

Black smoke billowed up over the west roof.

The barn.

"Rina!" he screamed, pushing himself to his feet. He ran toward the smoke and flames.

"Rook, wait!"

Deke's hand brushed his arm. He jerked away, pumping his legs faster.

Then Deke tackled him. He went down heavily, with Deke's arms locked around his legs.

Rook struggled, kicking. "Let go!"

Deke propelled himself up and over him, wrapping his arms around his shoulders in a bear hug. "Stop it, Rook!"

Rook heard a shout and the pounding of boots on the wet ground. He kicked again and tried to buck Deke off.

"You'll kill yourself. Taylor's men are checking it out."

Rook barely heard him. He bucked again.

"Get off me you son of a bitch! I've got to get to Rina!"

Chapter Four

Rook finally pushed Deke off of him, or Deke gave up and rolled away. He vaulted over Deke and up the porch steps, heading for the basement safe room. From the color and height of the smoke coming from the barn, he was sure nobody could get to the basement going that way. The fire was burning too hot.

He raced through the kitchen and down the basement stairs. With a giant leap off the bottom stair, he hurtled himself against the metal door, pounding with his right fist and groping for the intercom switch with his left.

He prayed that the wires hadn't been burned or shorted.

"Irina!" he shouted through the intercom's speaker. "Answer me!"

Nothing.

His scalp burned with fearful anticipation. Had the explosion compromised the steel mesh-reinforced walls of the safe room? Had she been hurt? Or worse, had the men gotten to her?

He took a deep breath and shouted the safe word. It was actually a phrase, made up one night as they lay in each other's arms after an hour of nonstop lovemaking. Loosely translated to English, the phrase meant "Come here often?"

"Irina, *Priyed'te s'uda chasto?*" he said carefully, enunciating the words the way he'd learned. He'd never been great with the language, although he could speak it. According to Irina, he always bungled the pronunciation. She'd laughed every time he spoke. He wished he could hear her laughter right now.

"*Priyed'te s'uda chasto,* Irina." He hit the door with his fist again, then spread his palm against the metal, ridiculously relieved to feel its chill against his skin. Rationally, he knew it was too thick to allow heat to penetrate, especially after only a few minutes, but he breathed easier anyway.

Please, he begged silently. *Answer me.*

"*Tol'ko—*" a choked voice crackled through the intercom. "*Tol'ko, kogda suda vhod'at.*"

Only when the ships come in.

Relief sent shivers across his scalp and the nape of his neck, where sweat prickled.

"Irina, thank God. Are you all right? Are you hurt? Can you unlatch the door?"

He heard her fumbling with the lock, then with a cold metallic snick, the latch sprung.

For an instant, he paused. She hadn't answered any of his questions. What if she wasn't alone? What if one of Novus's men was holding her?

But, no. She knew what to do. If she weren't safe, she'd have answered *Vse vrem'a,* "All the time," if she were compromised.

He swung the door open, expecting her to throw herself into his arms. But she didn't. She stood, a couple of feet back from the door, her arms wrapped around herself.

He examined her closely, looking for any sign of burns or injuries. She looked unhurt, but she was shivering.

"You're freezing. Dammit. I should have grabbed that blanket for you. Come here." He held out his arms.

She looked at his outspread hands, then met his gaze. Her eyes were wide and dilated with fright. "Is it safe?"

His embrace or the situation? "We've contained the attack."

Her gaze held his for an instant, then she pushed past him and went up the stairs.

He turned to follow her, but the straight, stiff line of her back in the silk dressing gown spoke volumes. In fact, she couldn't have been clearer if she'd shouted.

She didn't want his help, nor his comfort. He couldn't blame her. She'd managed for two years without it.

He was terrified that during that time she'd decided that being without him was easier than being with him.

He didn't take his eyes off her until she disappeared through the door at the top of the stairs and closed it, quietly but firmly.

He couldn't make it up to her for leaving her. All he could do was make sure that everything around her was safe. So he stepped through the metal door and looked around. She'd turned on the solar lights that were fed by panels on the roof of the cabin, so it was easy to see that this end of the basement was undamaged.

However, the smell of smoke and burned wood and rubber permeated the air, and forty feet away, at the other end of the room, he could see where the steel mesh that reinforced the basement walls was bare in several places. Whatever they'd use to blow up the barn, it had generated enough heat to incinerate the plywood.

The basement was slightly soundproofed by virtue of the reinforced walls and metal doors. Still, it must have been terrifying for her, down here alone, listening to the gunfire. He couldn't imagine what she'd gone through as the explosion ripped the roof off the barn and burned through the walls he'd assured her were impenetrable.

For all his training and experience, in the Air Force and afterward, it occurred to him that beneath it all he was a naive idiot, thinking that because he thought he'd made her safe, she actually was.

Worse, he'd expected her to blindly accept his decisions—expected her to trust her life to them.

When had he become so arrogant and self-delusional?

The door behind him opened.

"Rook?"

He heard Deke's voice in his ears and through the com unit at the same time.

"Yeah."

"I saw Irina." Deke's footsteps were light on the wooden stairs. For his size, he could move almost without a sound. He stepped up beside Rook. "She didn't seem to be hurt—"

"Not physically," Rook finished, wincing. "She's never going to trust me again." He started toward the other end of the room.

Deke muttered something as he walked beside him.

"What? You might as well say it out loud. It won't be anything I haven't already said to myself."

"Have you called yourself an arrogant prick? Because that's what I'm calling you."

"Actually, yeah."

"Good. With your vote, it's unanimous." Deke widened the distance between them as they came closer to the far wall.

The smell of burned wood and rubber grew stronger, as did the heat. The crackling of flames filled the silence.

"It took nearly losing Mindy to make me realize what's really important."

"I know what's important. Why do you think I did what I did?"

Deke snorted in disgust. "Yeah, you know what *you* think is important. Don't put Irina through what I put Mindy through." He moved to the south wall. "Damn, that was some explosion."

Rook stepped to his left, to the north side. "Yep. Took the whole roof off the front of the barn."

"Aw, man. Look at my car." Deke's SUV was in flames, and several other small fires were still burning.

The rental car Rook had parked near the safe-room door appeared untouched. He took a few steps closer and pulled a small, high-powered flashlight out of his pocket. The roof was still intact over this end of the building, and he saw very little damage.

A beam of light crossed his on the concrete floor. Deke was checking out the south side.

"The SUV's leaking gas," Deke said.

Rook trained his light beam on the same area where Deke's light was shining. "How close to the flames?"

"Close."

Then Rook saw it. A line of liquid trickling along the floor, from the smoldering SUV to the rental car. As he watched, the center of the line caught fire.

"The gas just caught," Deke said. "It's spreading in both directions." He flipped on his com unit. "Taylor?"

Rook flipped the switch on his own unit. He heard

static. These fancy new units didn't work that great underground.

For a second, he debated running to the vehicles and trying to stop the gasoline before it caught the rental car on fire, but even as he thought it, he saw the flames brighten.

Time had run out.

"Taylor!" Deke shouted. "Get your men away from the barn. It's about to blow!"

"Deke! Run!"

They both turned and ran.

IRINA HAD THE blanket wrapped around her shoulders, but no amount of external insulation was going to help the chill that sat like a block of ice inside her.

Deke had come in a few minutes ago. When he'd asked how she was doing, she'd merely shrugged. How did she answer that question? In the past week and a half, she'd abandoned her last shred of hope that Rook might still be alive, she'd almost lost two of her closest friends—Rook's oath brothers—to terrorists and she had come face-to-face with the man she'd finally, after two long years, accepted as dead.

Deke had studied her for a few seconds, a worried frown marring his rugged features, then asked her if Rook was still downstairs. Without waiting for an answer, he'd headed down there.

She hadn't moved. She still sat in the same position, waiting, not even sure why. What was she waiting for?

She supposed she should be doing something. Maybe making coffee? Or cooling bottles of water?

She'd neglected to buy the etiquette book that covered entertaining Secret Service agents who'd helped save their lives. Was she obligated to provide a full meal? Or just hors d'oeuvres? And was it impolite to exclude the attackers?

A near-hysterical chuckle escaped her lips. She didn't know how to receive a husband who'd pretended to be dead for two years. She couldn't possibly be expected to handle Secret Service and terrorists.

Leaning her elbows on the table, she pressed her face into her trembling hands. None of this seemed real. If she opened her eyes right now and found herself in her bed at Castle Ranch, still a widow, still essentially penniless, she wouldn't be surprised.

A coughing spell interrupted her wandering thoughts. Her throat burned, and the smell of smoke lingered in her nostrils. She stood, pulling the blanket more snugly around the flimsy red gown and negligee. She needed to wash her face and get dressed.

As she turned toward the sink, she felt something under her feet. Did the floor shake? A low rumble hit her ears, followed instantaneously by a deafening explosion.

The safe room!

"No!" she cried. *No!* She dropped the blanket and rushed toward the basement stairs.

"Rook!" His name tore from her raw throat.

Before she got to the door, it slammed open. She got a split-second glimpse of two looming figures.

Then a hard body collided with hers, propelling her backward. Rook's lean, muscled arms immediately grabbed her up.

His warm strength enveloped her. His hand cradled the back of her head and pressed her face into the hollow of his shoulder. Holding her. Protecting her.

She felt the soft cotton of his shirt beneath her palms. Then her fingertips encountered a thick, harsh ribbon of fabric. It was the nylon strap of the gun slung across his back. "Rook, are you okay? Please, please be okay."

His arms tightened around her and his voice hummed near her ear. "Shh. Shh. I'm here."

She doubled her fists in the material of his shirt, sobbing with relief. Right this second nothing mattered except that he was here. He was safe. He was alive.

"This is Cunningham." Deke's voice broke into her consciousness.

Rook stiffened.

"Yeah, we're fine. The two vehicles in the barn went up." Deke continued. "Everybody okay out there?"

Rook took his hand away from the back of her head and adjusted the com unit in his ear. He cocked his head as the arm embracing her slid to her shoulder.

"Good," he said, staring at a point beyond her left ear. His jaw flexed with tension. "Meet us in the front room to debrief."

Suddenly, as quickly as her fingers had noticed the difference in his soft shirt and the harsh gun strap, she sensed the difference in him. The hand touching her shoulder belonged to a soldier. A commander. Not a lover.

Her Rook, her sweet, safe love, was gone.

She pushed away. "I need to get dressed."

Deke stepped past them. "I'll sweep the rooms first."

She watched Deke's retreating back helplessly, wanting to yell at him not to go. *Stop leaving me alone with him.*

But it didn't matter. Rook might as well have been one of the nameless Secret Service agents swarming around the cabin. He was distant, detached, as he removed the com unit from his ear and put it in the box that sat on the counter. Then he swung the gun down from his shoulder and unloaded it and broke it down. He laid the parts on the table. From the small of his back, he retrieved a handgun and checked it, then slid it back into the waistband of his pants.

He did all this without looking at her or speaking to her. Then when it seemed he'd done everything he could think of to do to avoid talking to her or even looking her way, his gaze slid up to meet her eyes and he took a breath, as if about to speak.

But she had no idea what he'd been about to say, because at that instant Deke reappeared.

"Everything looks fine in here. You can go ahead, Irina." He stopped, his gaze moving from her to Rook. "Or—"

She spoke quickly. "I will dress and then make some coffee."

Rook shook his head. "No. No coffee. Join us in the front room. You need to know what we're going to do next."

"Fine," she said evenly. "I appreciate you including me—this time." Then she turned on her heel and left.

Wincing at the venom-laced words that lingered in the air, Rook watched her exit. She'd never been one to flaunt her beauty or her femininity. But her slender body was perfectly proportioned, beautifully formed. She walked like a princess, head held high, back straight, with no wasted movement. Yet to him, everything about her, even the slightest brush of her hair across her shoulders or the sweep of her eyelashes, was alluring, and profoundly sexy.

"Uh, Rook?"

He glanced sidelong at his friend. "What?"

"Taylor and his men are waiting in the front room for the debriefing."

When Rook walked in with Deke at his side, Dan Taylor was standing near the fireplace, dressed in his flak jacket and police windbreaker, speaking quietly to a fellow Secret Service agent and jotting notes on a spiral notepad. Two other agents were standing near the front door.

All of them straightened perceptibly as Rook and Deke entered. Taylor accepted a manila envelope from one of his men and stepped over.

"Colonel Castle. I have something here I'd like you to look at." He opened the envelope and pulled out several photos.

"That's Lieutenant Cunningham's guy who called himself Frank James. Along with a couple of the others found in the explosion of the old mine."

"Explosion?" Rook looked at Deke, who shrugged.

"I had to get Mindy to safety, and I didn't have a whole lot of options. I found some dynamite."

Dan continued. "Lieutenant Cunningham believes there were at least six men there, counting James, but the others were so badly burned we weren't able to re-cover enough for a definitive conclusion."

Rook took the photos and studied them.

As soon as he laid eyes on the first photo, his pulse hammered in his ears. That face—or one eerily similar—had haunted him across three continents. It was of a thin-faced man with dirty-blond hair. He was obviously dead, and although he'd been cleaned up for the photo, one side of his face was unrecognizable.

"This guy's a dead ringer for Novus Ordo, except for Novus's receding hairline."

"I *knew* it," Deke said. "The first time I laid eyes on him I knew I'd seen him before. He looks just like your sketch."

"He's got to be Novus's brother," Rook said, tapping the picture. "So that's how Ordo found out so much about all of us," Rook said. "His brother must have been here the whole time."

His temples throbbed. Was he finally close to identifying the terrorist—finally close to bringing down the man who was responsible for thousands of innocent deaths throughout the world? "Can we ID him? Fingerprints? Dental records? Publishing his photo?"

"We managed to get two prints off him. Dental records aren't as easy as you'd think. If you've got a tentative ID, you can use dental records to verify it. But it's like your CGI of Novus's face. With no place to start, it's almost impossible."

"Why not start here, in Crook County, with prints and dental records?" Rook asked. "Have you met FBI agent Adrian Schiff? Good. Contact him. Then, if nothing comes of the fingerprints or the DNA, maybe we can at least verify whether he's been living in this area."

Dan nodded. "I'll ask the local FBI to help with matching dental records. I like the idea of publishing the photo, too. It might flush out some of Ordo's followers.

Dan jotted some notes on his dog-eared pad. "I suspect you'd like to be there when your specialists see these photos?"

"And I want their reactions recorded. I want to study each one of their faces when they first see this." He handed the photos back to Dan.

"Now, sir. We need to get you and Mrs. Castle away from here. Two of my men have cleaned up the casualty and taken the prisoners in for interrogation. Two are securing the grounds and waiting for the local authorities."

Rook winced. "Do we have to involve the locals?"

"Yes, sir. That blast was visible for several miles. We're spinning it as an accident—gas line exploded, place was empty. We'll take care of the rental car."

It was a good plan. Simple. Two years ago, letting someone else take charge of anything wouldn't have been in Colonel Robert Kenneth Castle's playbook, but after spending all those months as an expatriate and fugitive, he found it disturbingly easy to acquiesce to the Secret Service agent.

"So how are you going to explain your presence?"

Deke spoke up. "I'm going to tell them I was on my way up here. They probably won't believe it was a coincidence, but there's not much they can do about it."

"After you're safely away, we'll have a talk with the sheriff."

"I want to know what you find out about the prisoners," Rook said. "And who set the explosive in the barn."

Taylor nodded. "My recommendation is that we first get you and Mrs. Castle to a safe location. We'll debrief there once we're done here."

"No. Take us back to the ranch."

"Sir, security at the ranch may have been compromised. Plus the specialists living on the grounds will know you're there."

Rook shook his head. "I have an obligation to my specialists—to everyone who works for me—to keep them safe. I trust you to take care of security at the ranch. At least, as Sun Tzu said, we'll be keeping our friends close and our enemies closer." He glanced at Deke.

"Yeah," Deke agreed, "but so will they."

IRINA BURIED her face in the white towel, breathing in its fresh, clean scent. She sent a silent blessing up for

Jocelyn Talltrees, a local woman who kept an eye on the cabin and cleaned it twice a month. She peered over the towel into the mirror. Eyes clouded with fear and worry stared back at her from a pale, drawn face.

She had dreamed of finding Rook alive. It was why she'd spent a fortune the past two years searching for any clue that might give her hope. If anyone had asked her, she'd have told them that finding him would make her the happiest person on the planet. That getting her husband back would make her life complete once again.

But as she'd already realized, this reality she found herself in was no dream come true. In fact, it was a nightmare.

The man who'd come back to her was a stranger. He reminded her of the man who'd saved her father from execution as a traitor to the former Soviet Union.

Her father was one of only eight people in the world who could approximate the level of genius of Albert Einstein. When the Soviet Union broke up, Leonid Tankien was branded a traitor because of his belief that scientific breakthroughs belonged to the whole world. In poor health, he'd been placed under house arrest in the care of his only daughter and sentenced to hang for treason.

The president of the United States sent a special extraction team in to rescue Tankien and his daughter. Rook was the commanding officer on that mission. Like a superhero, he'd swept in and rescued them and brought them to the United States.

The plane ride to Washington, D.C., was twenty-two hours long. Rook and Irina sat together while her father rested. By the time the plane landed at Dulles, Rook had transformed from terse military commander to gentle yet strong confidant, and Irina had fallen hopelessly in love.

Too bad for her.

She hung the towel over the rack and rolled down the sleeves of her white silk shirt. The black pants she'd fished out of the closet were a size too large now, but the cotton socks and hiking boots fit fine. She pulled her hair back from her face and refastened the rubber band with a wince.

For a brief moment she again buried her face in her hands and worked on controlling her breathing and swallowing the nausea that kept pushing at her throat.

Someone knocked on the bathroom door. When she opened it, she found herself staring up at Rook's handsome face.

He didn't even bother to try and raise a smile as his gaze raked her from head to toe. "We've got to go."

She nodded without speaking. Picking up a wool jacket, she glanced around for anything else she needed to take back to the ranch.

Rook took a step backward. "Now." He sent a brief glance around the room, then turned on his heel, leaving her to follow.

By the time Irina got to the front room, Rook and Special Agent Taylor were talking intensely in hushed tones, and Deke was pacing. He looked up as she came in.

"Hey, Irina. How're you doing?"

"Fine," she said shortly, and immediately regretted it. "I'm okay. How are you? And Rook?"

Deke shrugged. "He's afraid someone's going to get hurt. He's trying to work out a failsafe plan with Taylor."

Irina frowned. "Well, first, he is too late. He has already hurt a lot of people. And second, when will he learn there is no failsafe?"

"I'd think you'd know the answer to that question. You've been married to him for what? Six years now. He'll never learn that lesson. Your husband is the most idealistic SOB I've ever met. He actually believes that Good will win over Evil and that one man can make a difference."

Irina raised her brows. "And you don't?"

Deke ducked his head. "I'm still working on happy endings."

"Don't worry, Deke," she said, laying her hand on his arm. "You've got yours. Just make sure you don't forget what a precious gift you have in Mindy and— Oh, my gosh! You haven't named the baby yet, have you?"

A grin transformed Deke's features. "Oh, yes, we have. Deacon Robert Cunningham."

Irina stood on tiptoes and kissed his cheek. "Oh, Deke, I love it. I'm so happy for you."

He squeezed her shoulder. "Don't give up on Rook," he murmured. "He loves you more than life."

She stared at him as he straightened. His mouth quirked and he tilted his head, as if to say "But then, what do I know?"

"Irina." Rook's quelling voice hit her ears. His gaze snapped from her to Deke and back. "Ready to go?"

She lifted her chin a fraction. "Yes."

Out of the corner of her eye, she saw Deke turn and practically run for the door. She couldn't blame him. The ice between Rook and her was enough to freeze his nose off.

She stepped past Rook and let Special Agent Taylor escort her out the front door of the cabin and into a black SUV with heavily tinted windows.

As she waited uncomfortably for Rook to get in the seat beside her, Deke's earlier words echoed in her ears.

I'm still working on a happy ending.

She pressed her lips together in an effort to hold tears at bay.

At least you *are working on it,* she thought.

Chapter Five

Irina set the coffee carafe down and glanced at the clock over the door of Rook's basement office/ conference room. Eight-thirty in the morning. At this point she wanted more than anything to go to her suite and take a long, relaxing bath, then climb into bed and sleep for about a week, long enough to forget this nightmare.

But the nightmare wasn't over. In fact, it was only beginning. During the two-hour ride back to Castle Ranch, Deke had filled Rook in on the details of what had happened in the past two weeks.

He spoke calmly and matter-of-factly, as if he were presenting the details of a budget request, or outlining the advantages of one helicopter over another. But his deadpan delivery didn't soften the impact. Irina was shocked to hear all the details of what Matt had gone through, and all that Deke had endured.

The realization that every bit of it had been put into motion by her decision to call off her search for Rook was daunting and sobering.

Matt and Deke had put their lives on the line. Innocent people had been hurt and traumatized, because of her decision. People had died. Bad people—traitors, kidnappers, torturers. But still human beings.

By the time the SUV veered from the main road onto a gravel drive that led to a garage underneath Castle Ranch, Irina had been queasy with horror over the consequences of her innocent act. As soon as the garage door had closed, Rook had stepped over to the wall and pressed a code into an electronic keypad. A hidden door had opened into the room she now was standing in—another safe room. This one was a sound-proofed office suite, complete with a kitchen area and a bathroom. Even a minuscule elevator that ran to the large suite of executive offices on the main floor.

It had always baffled her that Rook, the bravest man she'd ever known, found it necessary to have so many safe rooms and secret hideouts. But now it made sense. Without such precautions, he'd already be dead, several times over.

Rook sat at the head of the conference table, with Deke and Special Agent Taylor to his right.

Irina watched along with them as the other special-ists came in.

Per Agent Taylor's instructions, the agents were brought down one at a time. Matt was brought in first.

His face was as pale as the straps on his arm sling. Purplish shadows ran under his eyes. When he saw Rook, he swayed, grabbing the back of a chair to steady himself. But he recovered and greeted Rook with a big grin before lowering himself gingerly into the seat to Rook's left. Irina caught the meaningful glance he sent toward Deke, and she saw the infinitesimal movement of Deke's shoulders.

Irina felt indignant on Matt's behalf. Rook shouldn't have made him come. He was obviously still too weak from surgery. From the looks of him, he probably shouldn't have been discharged yet. After all, he'd almost died up on that mountain top fighting for Aimee and her little boy's lives.

The next specialist to arrive was Aaron Gold. A red scrape above his right ear spoke to his brush with death. The sniper's bullet had missed his brain by a fraction of an inch.

Aaron's dark eyes behind his rimless glasses glittered and his face went ashen when his gaze lit on Rook, sitting at the head of the table.

"Colonel!" he gasped. "You're— Oh, my God!" He shook his head. "We all thought you were—"

"Dead," Rook responded. "I know."

Aaron nodded eagerly. Pink spots appeared in his cheeks. "This is unbelievable. I'm— What happened? Where have you been? Are you all right?"

Rook nodded. "I'm fine. Have a seat, Aaron. We've got a lot to talk about."

Aaron's eyes darted around the table as he sat. "Did you know about this?" he asked Deke.

Deke shook his head.

Aaron started to say something else, but at that moment the door opened again and Rafiq Jackson was standing there, leaning on crutches. His right pant leg was slit and his thigh was bandaged.

Irina turned her attention to Rook. He hadn't met Rafe, and she wanted to know what his first impression of the young man was. She'd never gotten to know Aaron very well. He was quiet and introverted. But she liked Rafe a lot. Maybe because he was the only member of the team that *she'd* hired. Or maybe because he was outgoing and funny and he seemed to have less to hide than either Aaron or Brock.

When she looked back at Rafe, he smiled. "Good morning, Irina," he said with a nod. Then his deep brown eyes slid to Deke and he nodded again. He planted the crutches in front of him and, looking down, swung forward a step.

"Rafe," Deke said. "Meet Rook Castle."

Rafe's smile froze on his face. He stared at Deke for a second before turning toward the head of the table. Then, much like Aaron, his eyes widened and his face drained of color. He swallowed, opened his mouth, closed it and then opened it again.

"Mr. Castle. I mean, Colonel Castle. I—I'm—"

Rook waited.

"This is a true honor, sir. I've always regretted that I never got to meet you. I've been— It's been a privilege to work here." He stood stiffly, his knuckles white on the crutch handles. "I must say, I'm stunned."

Rook nodded. "I'm seeing a lot of that today."

Rafe's gaze turned back to Irina and his brows raised slightly. "I'm certain of that, sir. Mrs. Castle, may I help you with the coffee?"

She shook her head. "No, thank you." She intercepted an irritated glance from Rook. He'd told her to forget the hostess duties and concentrate on the debriefing, but she'd needed something to do. Otherwise she was afraid she might give in to panic and start screaming.

Rafe took both crutches in one hand and lowered himself into a chair, wincing. Irina quelled the urge to go around the table and take his crutches before he dropped them. He had no business being out of the hospital yet, either.

Two down and one to go. She glanced up at the clock again. Eight-thirty in the morning. Where was

Brock? Usually he was the first one awake in the mornings, the first one to arrive at a meeting, and the last one to turn in at night. Had Rook left him until last for a reason?

The doorknob turned and Brock came in. He looked like he always did. Crisp and neat—military neat. His shoes were polished, his slacks were pressed and his shirt was dazzlingly white. His good eye slid from face to face, until he met Rook's gaze.

Brock went still, reminding Irina of a champion bird dog on point. His body was perfectly balanced, his senses razor sharp. He exuded focus and concentration. No matter what might be required, he was ready.

Rook's head went up a fraction and his lips curved slightly. "Brock," he said.

"Colonel Castle." Brock nodded once. Nothing else. No effusive greeting. No exclamation of joy that Rook was alive. Merely that simple acknowledgment.

Yet she saw his hand twitch at his side. An odd reaction from the ex-Navy Seal whose survival had depended more than once on his self-control. Rook had told her stories about him. She glanced at Rook, wondering if he'd noticed, but his face revealed nothing.

Brock sat next to Rafe and rested his clasped hands on the table. They were steady, motionless now.

Irina picked up the tray of coffee-filled mugs and set it in the middle of the table.

The men reached for the mugs—even Rook, and the small wrinkles between his brows smoothed out a bit as he took a long swig of the hot drink. His reluctant appreciation sent a little flare of triumph through her.

After taking the last mug herself, she sat in the empty chair to Special Agent Taylor's right. She wrapped her fingers around the warm mug and took a sip. It *was* good coffee, which made her wonder who kept the coffee down here fresh and the pot and mugs dust free.

She realized Rook was speaking. With an effort, she concentrated on what he was saying.

"I'm sure you all have a lot of questions," he said, looking from Matt to Aaron, from Rafe to Brock.

Rafe laughed quietly. Aaron and Matt nodded, and Brock didn't blink or move a muscle.

"Well, right now, we've just come from a confrontation with several individuals whom I'm sure were sent by Novus Ordo." He nodded toward the right side of the table, where Deke, Special Agent Taylor and Irina sat. "So I apologize, but there's no time for discussion about me and where I've been. Deke or I will fill you in on a need-to-know basis."

He leaned forward. "What we need to talk about right now is what happened this morning, and what precautions we need to take at this point. What I will say as a preface, is that I'm here because of everything that's happened during the past two weeks. I look around this table. It's impossible to miss that each one of you has been injured because of me. I regret that, and I regret that I can't give you each time off to heal."

He waved his hand. "Don't bother shaking your heads. I know, and I appreciate it. All of you have met Special Agent Dan Taylor, right? He'll tell us about the prisoners. This is our first debrief, so I'd appreciate it if you'd hold any questions until Dan is done. Dan?"

"Yes, sir. Colonel Castle and Lieutenant Cunningham faced three attackers at a facility owned by Colonel Castle. We don't know at this point if the three were the only ones. Explosives destroyed the barn and two vehicles on the property. No casualties were found in the rubble. The three could have set the explosives prior to attacking, or they could have had help. We have two of the men in custody. The third was a casualty on site. No evidence of other accomplices."

Taylor flipped a page in his small spiral-bound notebook. "We had to notify the sheriff over there, because of the visibility of the explosion. We'll brief you as needed about any contact you may have with that office. The Crook County medical examiner took charge of the body of the single casualty. The other two are in custody in the former Treasury Department building in Sundance. I have two men guarding them, but we haven't had a chance to question them yet."

"Do you have photos?" Rook asked.

"Yes, sir." Taylor nodded to the Secret Service agent standing at the exit door. The agent retrieved a small manila envelope from his inside jacket pocket and handed it over.

Rook glanced quickly at the three photos, then shuffled them and scrutinized them more closely.

"We found a vehicle hidden in brush a mile south of the cabin. It's a junker with expired tags. We're tracing the last owner, but odds are it was bought or stolen from a junkyard. I don't expect there to be any way to trace it."

Rook nodded. He handed the photos to Matt and gestured for him to pass them around.

No one said a word as the photos changed hands. Rook watched as Matt, Aaron, Rafe and Brock examined the pictures.

"If any of you recognize anyone," Rook said, "speak up."

Dan jotted a note on his pad, looked at it for a moment, then leaned over and whispered something behind his hand to Deke. Deke cut his eyes over at Dan and then nodded.

For the first time, Irina noticed how Dan was dressed. His slacks were perfectly tailored and she wouldn't risk a dollar betting against that white dress shirt being handmade. His expensive clothes didn't fit with the dog-eared dollar store notepad and cheap mechanical pencil he carried.

"While you're looking at pictures, I've got three more for you to see." He gestured to the guard again and was handed another manila envelope.

"I've e-mailed all of these to our computer expert in D.C. She'll run them against our known terrorist database for a facial recognition match. I've ordered DNA and fingerprints and Special Agent Schiff has requested top priority for the results."

Dan handed the envelope to Rook, who looked at each one carefully. He glanced at Deke and then returned the pages to the envelope and handed them to Matt, who was seated directly to his left.

Irina knew the photos were of the man who'd named himself Frank James and two of the terrorists who'd worked with him on Mindy's kidnapping. And she knew the specialists' reactions were being recorded. She watched carefully, wondering if she'd be able to spot any reaction.

Matt took a quick glance through them and handed them on to Aaron, who seemed to know he was being scrutinized as he studied the faces. He quickly passed them on to Rafe and shook his head at Dan.

"Nothing. I mean, there for a minute I thought I recognized that first guy, but no."

"I've never seen them, either." Rafe handed the envelope to Brock. "You're up," he said, smiling.

Brock glanced through the small stack of photos, shook his head and laid them down on the table. "Who are these guys?"

"They're the men who were after Deke in the mine."

He looked at Deke. "That first guy is the one who called himself Frank James?"

Deke nodded.

"That's interesting." Brock slid the folder across the table to Dan.

"Interesting?" Dan repeated.

"Jesse James was the more famous of the brothers, but a lot of scholars think Frank was the real brains."

"That's what he said," Deke remarked. "I goaded him about naming himself after the *brother* of an outlaw, and he said Frank was smarter."

Irina kept her attention on Rafe and Aaron. Rafe was following the conversation with his typical engaging fervor. Aaron was listening, but as was usual for him, he didn't show much emotion.

Dan tapped the edge of the folder on the tabletop. "Do you think that's significant?" he asked, directing his question to Rook.

"You mean, do I think that it's a clue to Novus Ordo's identity?" He nodded. "I wouldn't be surprised."

At the mention of the terrorist, both Aaron and Rafe tensed. But then, so did almost everyone else at the table. The notable exception was Brock. Still, he was the one that had introduced the conjecture.

"I want to see the prisoners in the flesh," Rook said. "How soon can you arrange that?"

"If you don't mind, sir, I'd appreciate it if we could keep them isolated for at least twenty-four hours."

Rook looked like he was going to object. Irina knew he didn't find it easy to acquiesce to someone else's authority. Especially someone like Agent Taylor, who was younger and much less experienced than he.

Deke cleared his throat quietly.

Rook's chin lifted and his eyes narrowed slightly. "Fine. Make sure you understand that I'm not only concerned about the safety of my family and my employees. This is also a matter of national security."

"Yes, sir," Taylor said. "The White House made it very clear that this team's mission was to keep you and your family safe and to gather every bit of information we can about Novus Ordo. Oddly enough, Ordo seems to have disappeared around the same time you did. The destruction of the chemical munitions plant in Mexico two years ago was his last known attack.

"Homeland Security has ramped up its surveillance of audio and electronic transmissions throughout the world, and we've upped scrutiny and troop availability in the Far East, especially the areas that join Afghanistan, Pakistan and China."

Irina doubted anyone in the room, except maybe Deke, noticed a difference in Rook's attitude, but she had. A nearly imperceptible relaxation of the tension across his forehead told her that he was impressed with Agent Taylor.

"So how long have you been on this assignment, Taylor?"

"A month, sir. However, most of the team has been here since right after you disappeared."

Rook blinked. He was surprised. Another thing he hadn't known.

"A month. So I can assume you're not totally up to speed on the situation?"

Taylor's mouth quirked almost imperceptibly. "More today than yesterday. As Lieutenant Cunningham told you, he briefed me after he'd spoken to you. I was originally assigned here when the agent in charge had to take bereavement leave. At that time I was told we were guarding your wife, because of your connection with Novus Ordo and the international involvement and implications in your…death. That's the extent of my knowledge."

"Fine," Rook said curtly, setting down his mug. For a few short seconds he stared at the surface of the coffee, or at his hand—Irina couldn't be sure. "It's probably as good a time as any to bring all of you up-to-date."

He raised his gaze and looked at each specialist. "Four years ago, I was asked by the president to go into Mahjidastan to rescue Travis Ronson." He sent an apologetic glance in Aaron's direction.

Aaron nodded once, gravely.

"We lost Norman Gold on that mission—Aaron's dad. He died a hero. Matt and Deke were with the mission. Brock was holding things together back here, Aaron hadn't joined Search and Rescue at that time. He was still in school."

Dan nodded eagerly. "I remember that incident. Ronson's oldest son."

"Oldest of five."

Rook nodded. "He was a Navy fighter pilot and was shot down. Ronson is a close friend of the former president's, and he couldn't stand to think that Fred might lose another son. So we went in after him."

"That was you who pulled off that rescue." The awe in Taylor's voice was palpable.

Rook nodded at Deke. "We had intel that Ronson was being held by the terrorist who had bombed a nuclear plant in India, killing thousands. Deke—Lieutenant Cunningham—flew a grid over the entire area, searching for signs of their camp. It's damn rocky up there, but Deke spotted a small campfire and some tents. Before he could get away, Novus shot his helicopter down and took him captive, too." Rook finished his coffee.

Irina reached for his cup, but he checked her with a sharp gesture.

"At that time, micro-GPS locators embedded under the skin were investigational. Deke had one of the first. Luckily it worked. We extracted Ronson and him without any further casualties to our side, but—"

The tension and expectancy in the room was palpable. Dan Taylor leaned forward. Rafe and Aaron were both staring at Rook, entranced.

"I came face-to-face with Novus Ordo."

"Without his mask," Taylor breathed.

Irina almost smiled. The special agent, who had to be four or five years younger than Rook's thirty-three, was obviously starstruck by him. She could understand why. Rook had a presence about him. He was larger than life. Heroic.

"I saw his face and he almost killed me. He managed to grab my dog tags. So I can identify him, and he knows who I am."

"So faking your own assassination was—"

"A well-meaning but foolish attempt to stop Ordo from targeting me and my family."

Irina wanted to believe that. She *wanted* to believe everything Rook said. But in all the time they'd been married, the one thing she'd never had was Rook's complete trust. He seemed to view everyone as a potential enemy—even her. And this moment was no exception. He didn't glance toward her as he spoke. He didn't look at anyone. He stared at his clasped hands.

Matt sat up gingerly. "It was a good plan, until Irina was forced to abandon her search. Her decision was innocent, but Ordo had obviously been watching her for the past two years. He was alerted. He couldn't afford to believe that she'd stopped merely because of financial problems, or because she'd gotten proof that he was dead. Ordo had to operate on the assumption that she'd found him."

Hearing those words in Matt's low voice sent a shard of guilt stabbing into Irina's breast. She could never tell anyone about the surprising feeling of relief she'd felt when she'd finally made the decision to stop putting money into the futile effort of proving her dead husband wasn't dead.

The truth was, after two years of hanging on to that tattered shred of hope, finally letting go had been a relief.

Chapter Six

She turned back toward the coffeepot as her face heated with shame. She felt Rook's eyes burning into her back.

"So, clever bastard that he is, Ordo managed to put a complex plan together in a matter of hours," Deke threw in. "I don't care if he did have two years to work on it, the plan he devised shows he's a genius. The deadliest mistake we can make is to underestimate him."

Irina poured water into the coffeemaker and turned it on.

"I left Mahjidastan within twenty minutes of hearing from Irina," Matt said, "yet Ordo still managed to have me followed and contact one of his agents in the U.S. to kidnap baby William. He knew about my best friend's widow and her son. And he knew I'd drop everything to save them."

When Irina turned around, it was obvious that Rook was listening intently, although his expression was stony. She could tell this was the first time he'd heard all the details of what had happened. She studied his face. It was impossible to tell if he was affected by the knowledge that she'd searched for him all that time.

He really had cut himself off totally—and he'd done it for her safety.

No, not her safety. *The nation's.*

Rook's jaw muscle ticced. "Novus has made it his mission to know everything about the brotherhood, so—"

"Excuse me, sir. Brotherhood?"

Rook's face lightened for an instant, then sobered again. "Matt, Deke, me, and Bill Vick. When we were around nine or ten years old, the four of us went on a mountain adventure and nearly died when a storm blew in. A brave man named Arlis Hanks lost his life rescuing us. Hanks was a combat rescue officer in the Air Force during Vietnam. Their motto is *That others may live.* We took an oath to live our lives by the same creed. I started Black Hills Search and Rescue to pay forward what Arlis Hanks did for us."

Dan scribbled something on his notepad. "Where's Bill Vick?"

Matt spoke up. "Bill Vick was my best friend. He died last year."

"And how does Novus know about this oath you took?"

Deke shrugged. "He doesn't. But he's figured out that each one of us would give our life to save the others."

"Why we do what we do doesn't mean anything to you," Rook stated. "Just be aware that Novus Ordo has killed who knows how many people to protect his identity. And he will again."

Rook paused, watching the effect of his words on those gathered in the room. Brock and Aaron knew about the mission to rescue Ronson. Brock's reaction was exactly what Rook had expected. No sign of surprise or interest. Aaron had joined Black Hills

Search and Rescue just weeks after the rescue, so he knew most of the story.

Rafe appeared spellbound, like a kid in the presence of his favorite superhero.

Rook turned his attention to the Secret Service agent. Agent Dan Taylor was an interesting man. Six feet tall and well-built, he seemed more mature than his years. And something Rook said had affected him. Quickly replaying his recent remarks, Rook decided that it must have been the mention of the brotherhood. He filed that piece of information away.

Taylor turned to Matt. "Lieutenant Parker, you said you were in Mahjidastan when Mrs. Castle called you?" he asked.

Matt nodded. "Following up on a rumor that an American had traveled there recently. If Novus had a tail on me, it was a damn good one. I never caught the guy. But obviously, he knew the instant I left. Apparently knew I was there and was keeping an eye on me, so he had me followed back here to Wyoming. Then he kidnapped Bill Vick's widow's seven-month-old son in an effort to capture me."

"But his plan didn't work." Deke tossed back the last of his coffee and set the mug down on the table with a thud. "Any more than his plan to take my wife hostage to force me to reveal where Rook was. And now he's after Irina."

Taylor assessed Deke and Matt.

Rook knew what he was thinking. "You're wondering why Novus didn't try something more direct, like stopping Matt before he got on that plane, or going after Deke instead of capturing his ex-wife."

Dan shrugged. "I'm guessing he knew they wouldn't talk, with nothing at stake but their own lives.

I've got to agree with Lieutenant Cunningham. Novus has to be extremely intelligent to plan and carry out all this on such short notice."

"Oh, he is." Rook nodded. "But as Deke said, it's likely he's had tentative plans in the works for months—probably since I disappeared. Still, not only did he underestimate Deke and Matt, he underestimated Aimee Vick and Mindy Cunningham, as well. Even so, he accomplished his ultimate goal. He managed to flush me out. Now that he knows I'm alive—"

"He'll do whatever he has to do to destroy the man who exposed his true face," Deke said, then paused, looking at Rook.

"What about the CGI?"

Rook's gaze met Matt Parker's. He sent him a nearly imperceptible nod.

Matt stood and stepped over to a fireproof safe.

Dan's gaze followed him. "You have a computer-generated image of Novus Ordo? Who did the drawing?"

"The CIA, using my descriptions."

"No hits?"

Rook shook his head. "Not even close."

Her husband's disgusted tone reminded Irina of how obsessed he'd been with finding the man whose face he'd seen. The lengthy phone calls with CIA, Homeland Security and other government officials, the numerous trips he made to Washington to look at photo arrays. The memories weren't fond ones.

They'd married a few months after Rook's rescue of her father, six years ago. The first two years she spent learning to trust and love him and his country.

Then, right when she was becoming comfortable in his love, he'd gone on that mission to save Travis Ronson and seen Novus Ordo's face. So the next two years were lonely, as he spent most of his time obsessed with identifying the terrorist. And of course, these past two years she'd spent alone.

Right now, standing here, watching her husband and the two men he trusted most in the world, assessing the nature and the source of the threat against their lives, it occurred to her that she'd have to dig awfully deep to unearth *any* fond memories.

She held up the fresh carafe of coffee and glanced around the table. In response to the nods, she refilled mugs.

Matt closed and locked the safe, handed a manila folder to Rook and returned to his seat.

Rook forced his hands not to shake as he slid the photo out of the folder, just enough to see the subject's eyes and nose.

Novus Ordo. Latin for "New Order."

A surge of anger washed over him, surprising him. He hadn't expected to react so strongly to the drawing. After all, the man's face was engraved into his brain. He didn't need a computer-generated image to remind him of what he looked like.

Nor did he need to look at the photo of Frank James to know that the two men were brothers—that they could be twins.

But he wanted to. "Hand me that photo of Frank James."

Dan picked up the folder and passed it to him. Rook held the two images side by side.

No question. If they could get a hit off James's prints or DNA, maybe they could finally identify Novus.

He handed the two pictures to Dan, who grabbed them eagerly.

"Pass them to Rafe when you're done," Rook said.

Then he turned to Jackson. "You haven't seen the drawing yet, have you?"

Rafe shook his head, his gaze following the manila folder. "No, sir, I have not," he said in his faintly British accent.

Dan stared at the two images. Irina looked over his shoulder. The resemblance between the drawing put together from Rook's description and the photograph of Frank James was amazing.

"This is Novus Ordo?" Dan sounded stunned.

No one bothered to answer him.

"He's American!" he exclaimed, then immediately corrected himself. "I mean, he's—Anglo. Caucasian?"

"Yeah," Deke said flatly. "We know."

"And he and James are dead ringers!"

Rook nodded. "Except that Novus is losing his hair."

"And in all this time, the CIA couldn't find him?"

"I'd have done it differently, but the CIA felt that starting with a narrow sample and gradually widening would eliminate even the slightest margin of error. So rather than publishing the sketch, they chose to start with criminal records."

"Mug shots," Dan offered.

Rook nodded. "I looked at every ugly, two-bit criminal in Wyoming and the surrounding states. And nothing. Which didn't surprise me. My guess is that when we do find out who Novus Ordo is, he'll turn out to be some formerly mild-mannered guy with no criminal record. The kind who's easily swayed by whatever latest fad religion or cause comes along."

"Like Ted Kaczynski?"

Rook nodded. "Probably never got a parking ticket. I wouldn't have started with criminals, but I guess they had to start somewhere."

"What was their next step?"

"Driver's license photos. But I'm guessing that once I disappeared, they suspended the search. I mean, what would be the point? As far as they were concerned, I was dead."

"So not even the CIA was aware of your plan?" Dan asked.

Rook felt an overwhelming urge to defend his decision. But he suppressed it. What was done was done. No matter whether he'd made the right decision or not, he had to live with it. He sent the young agent a quelling glare. "No."

Dan's face reddened and he nodded. "Have you contacted them since you returned?"

"Agent Taylor, I flew into Casper yesterday, using a counterfeit identity I set up prior to my disappearance. When I'd thanked the attendant as I walked off the plane, that was the first time I'd spoken to anyone in the U.S. in two years."

Dan looked surprised. "No one? No one at all?"

Exasperated, Rook shook his head. "Not my wife. Not Deke. No one. It would have been too dangerous."

He glanced briefly at Irina, but she appeared to be involved in stirring her coffee. She was tired. He could read her exhaustion in the slope of her back and neck. She'd changed from the sexy red silk gown to a white shirt and pants that were too big for her. Even so, they didn't hide the enticing curve of her back or her vulnerable nape.

Dan lowered his gaze to his notepad. After a second of awkward silence, he took a deep breath. "I believe that's all the questions I have at this time—for the specialists."

Rook dragged his attention away from his wife. The

look in Agent Taylor's eye and the inflection in his voice told him a lot. He wanted to talk about Rook's employees.

Rook nodded his understanding. "Brock, Aaron, Rafe. Thanks for your time and input. Agent Taylor and I have a few more things to discuss. You're dismissed."

Once the three of them had exited and the door was closed, Rook turned to Matt. "You don't have to stay for this. Deke or I can fill you in later."

Matt smiled. "Not a chance. I'm here. I want to hear everything."

"Great." He turned back to Dan. "You have more questions?"

"I understand from Deke—Lieutenant Cunningham—that there's strong reason to suspect one of your employees of feeding information to Novus."

"That's what he told me. Deke?"

Deke leaned back in his chair and raked his fingers through his hair. "Dan, you've heard the short version."

Dan nodded. "Your helicopter was sabotaged. I'd like to hear how. Who could have done it. And who couldn't have. I've viewed the security disks. I'm assuming that whoever did the tampering knew how to avoid being recorded."

Deke nodded. "That's right. As for the how: Someone drained all the oil *and* tampered with the oil gauge, so it had to be someone with a little technical knowledge," Deke said. "I followed my usual start-up routine. I'd checked all the fluid levels the night before. I did my walk-around—to make sure there were no leaks. Then I did a visual check of the mechanics. I started the engine and checked all the gauges. But when I tried to take off, the motor seized." Deke rubbed his eyes. "Draining the oil is a pretty simple matter, if you know where the drain plug is. But doing it in the short time frame they had to work within, without spilling a drop? That takes more patience, skill and attention to detail than most people have."

"So which one of your specialists has those traits?"

Deke shook his head. "All of them."

He leaned back in his chair and raked his fingers through his hair again. "I've worked with each of these three guys and found them competent and trustworthy. Until my bird was sabotaged, I'd have said I could trust each of them with my life, but obviously I was wrong there. I've gone over everything I know about them, and I can give you at least one reason to suspect each one."

"*At least* one? Which ones have more than one?"

While Dan was speaking, Rook stood and stepped over to where Irina was sitting, near the coffeepot. She'd been getting more and more pale, and he could tell by the way her skin stretched across her cheekbones how exhausted she was. He put a hand on her shoulder and leaned down. The scent of gardenias wafted past his nostrils from her hair.

"Why don't you go upstairs? There's no reason for you to sit through this."

She stiffened under his touch. "I'm fine," she hissed.

"It's obvious you're not."

"I thought you wanted me to hear everything." Her voice was still icy.

"I can brief you tomorrow—or Deke can, if you don't trust me."

"I'm. Fine."

Rather than make any more of a scene than they'd already made, Rook gave up and went back to his seat.

She wasn't about to give him a break. Not that he deserved one, but it still hurt.

He pushed his thoughts back behind the steel wall of his heart, where he kept things he didn't have time to deal with, or didn't want to.

Behind him, Deke was filling Dan in on the specialists, and Rook needed to be listening.

"The one person I've always known I can count on is Brock O'Neill. He's been around the longest. He's a former Navy Seal, got a disability discharge when he lost his eye on a mission."

"He lives on the ranch?"

"Sort of," Deke said.

Dan's brows went up. "Sort of? What does that mean?"

Deke shifted. "He's here during the week."

"And on weekends?"

Irina caught the look that passed between Deke and Rook. She'd seen it before. The two of them sometimes communicated in ways that she didn't understand.

Deke turned back to the Secret Service agent. "We don't know."

"You don't—?"

"His weekends are his own. He doesn't have to tell us where he goes."

"But you have an opinion, right?"

"Nope. Not me."

Irina's gaze shot involuntarily to Rook's. She knew as soon as her eyes met his that he was thinking the same thing she was: Deke wasn't telling everything he knew.

She knew that Brock disappeared most weekends. He'd always done it, and Rook had always allowed it, unless Brock was on an active mission. She'd never asked Rook where the ex-Navy Seal went on his own time, and Rook had never volunteered the information.

Dan intercepted her gaze and started to speak, then stopped and mentally regrouped. He jotted a note on his pad, then looked up. "What's his specialty? What was the last job he did for Black Hills Search and Rescue?"

"Brock took over my job as mission coordinator when I took over Rook's position," Deke said. "He's got expertise in explosives, as well as several other areas. But at heart, he's a tracker. He's half Sioux Indian, so I suppose tracking is in his blood. He can track over ground, in water and over rock. Best I've ever seen."

"How can you be sure you can trust him?"

"Because I know him. He wouldn't betray his country."

"You said he's Sioux. Maybe he doesn't recognize the United States of America as his country."

Anger flared in Deke's eyes. To his credit, he didn't say anything.

Irina understood. It was one thing to speak in generalities about someone feeding information to Novus Ordo. It was quite another to specifically target each trusted employee.

"Brock's last assignment was a missing-child case," she offered. "A mother and her two boys went on a picnic in a supposedly safe camping area. The younger, a six-year-old, disappeared."

"He had a child locator on." Deke took over the story. "But the locator was found at the bottom of a ravine, smeared with blood consistent with the boy's blood type. The child hasn't been found."

Dan shook his head. "Sad story. Has that affected his work?"

"No," Deke said.

"I think he's still looking for the child," Irina put in. "I think that is what he does on his time these days. I tried to tell him to let it go. But he is a stubborn man, and I'm afraid he may have developed feelings for the mother. In any case, that's about the time my accountant started warning me about finances, so that was the last pro bono case we took."

"And when was that?"

She thought for a second. "Two months ago."

Dan turned back to Deke. "What about the other two?"

Rook spoke up. "Aaron Gold is our computer and communications expert. He's young, only twenty-three. His dad was a good friend of mine. One of my mentors. Like I told you, he died on that mission under my command." He rubbed his face.

"Aaron followed in his dad's footsteps and got his degree in computer engineering while he was in the Air Force. I hired him for his computer knowledge, and because I felt responsible for him after his dad's death."

"Think he resents you for taking his dad away from him?"

Rook shook his head. "I'd have said no, but—"

"Aaron was pretty shook up when he heard about Rook's death. I think he thought of Rook as a father figure," Deke put in. "Oh, and he does live here on the ranch, in the guesthouse."

Dan glanced down at his notepad. "And Rafiq Jackson. What kind of name is that?" He looked up at Rook, who shook his head and gestured toward Deke.

"Irina hired him several months ago. He was born

in England." Deke sat back in his chair and crossed his arms. "He's our terrorism and language expert."

"So he's not an American citizen?" Dan asked.

Deke nodded tersely. "Yeah, he is. Naturalized. He's never had military service, but he studied math in the U.S. and worked for NSA until he got sick of government bureaucracy—his words."

"Rafiq—what kind of name is that? It sounds—"

"His mother is from Saudi Arabia. His father is British."

Dan nodded. "Anything else out of the ordinary about him? Other than his heritage, I mean?"

Irina responded. "He was unemployed for two years after he quit NSA. According to his CV, he took a trip around the world. I hired him for his language skills."

"You advertised for a language expert?"

"No. We didn't advertise."

"So, how did you know about him?"

Rook sat forward. He wanted to know the answer to that, too.

Irina spoke then. "We received his CV in the mail," she answered Dan. "We were not advertising, but when we saw his credentials, we called him in."

"We both liked what we saw," Deke said.

"I can show you his introductory letter," Irina continued. "His education and experience were impressive. And he said he had always wanted to work search and rescue."

Her voice quivered slightly at the end. Rook understood why. She was questioning her decision. Had she unknowingly hired a terrorist? She had good instincts about people, but sometimes her feelings got in the way of her better judgment.

He turned his gaze to Deke.

"I vetted him," Deke said. "All the way back to Hampstead Garden, England, to his birth records."

"So tell me, why does a search-and-rescue operation need a terrorism and language specialist?"

Deke sent the Secret Service agent an exasperated look. "Because this particular search-and-rescue operation is on Novus Ordo's short list."

Chapter Seven

"Black Hills Search and Rescue wasn't created to be a typical search-and-rescue service like so many who operate here in the mountain states. You might say our scope is pretty broad."

Rook clasped his hands on the table. "Dan, I know you've only been here a month, but you were assigned here by the president. I'm certain you know the answers to many if not all of these questions you're asking." He paused long enough for the silence to become uncomfortable.

Dan didn't take the bait. He sat still, staring at his pad, waiting for Rook to continue.

"Given our customers, it makes perfect sense to me that Deke and Irina would hire a language and terrorism expert."

"Yes, sir," Dan replied. "I'm not questioning the decision. I'm merely interested in finding out why Rafiq Jackson sent his CV *here*."

The question hung there in the air until Irina spoke.

"Are you saying this is the only place he sent it?"

Dan's head turned sharply in her direction.

Rook nodded to himself. Excellent question.

After an instant of silence, Dan nodded. "I'll check." He flipped a page. "Okay. Moving on, tell me about Fiona Hathaway."

Irina looked surprised. "Fiona? How did you get her name?"

"Same as all the other specialists. From your assistant, Pam Jamieson."

"Fiona is on a leave of absence—maternity leave. Has been for the past two months. She has nothing to do with this."

"Fiona had a baby?" Rook was surprised. She'd never seemed like the type to want children.

Irina nodded.

"She was a major in the Air Force," Deke supplied. "Commanded a medical reserve unit until she retired four years ago. She's also a cartography expert. Her unit was deployed to Afghanistan, and she returned with medals for bravery, although there were some rumors circulating that she may not have deserved them."

"Oh, yeah? Why not?"

"I didn't ask," Rook said. "Fiona informed me about the rumors and assured me they weren't true."

Dan jotted down a quick note, probably to request the information from the Air Force.

"Who's the father of her baby?"

"Never asked that, either."

Dan nodded and flipped backward several pages.

"So that's four specialists. They're the only people, other than you, who could have access to the kind of information we know has been given to Ordo?"

Rook, Deke and Matt all nodded.

"But Fiona has a really good alibi," Irina pointed out. "She was in the hospital in labor when the helicopter was sabotaged."

Dan looked at each of them in turn. "So who is your traitor? Brock O'Neill, Aaron Gold or Rafiq Jackson?"

No one spoke.

Rook rubbed his palm down his cheek to his chin. "It could be any one of the three."

"WHAT ARE YOU planning to do? Hide down here in the basement all day?"

Irina didn't answer Rook's question. She didn't even look at him. She didn't have to. Even with her back turned, she knew exactly what he was doing. He was leaning against the door frame with his arms crossed and his jaw set. He was angling for a fight. It was how he always argued. Closed off. Irritatingly rational. And with a subtle undertone of sarcasm that could sting like an angry hornet.

As frustrating as his superior attitude was, she felt a disturbing nostalgia. She'd even missed this.

She'd stayed behind when the meeting broke up, using the dirty coffeepot and cups as an excuse, although what she'd really wanted to do was avoid the awkwardness of going upstairs at Rook's side. She wished she could slip into her suite and lock the door and avoid the question of where he would sleep.

She ran the coffee carafe under the hot water tap one more time and set it on the drain board in the small kitchen, then started on the mugs. Maybe if she ignored him long enough, he'd give up and go away.

"Irina, we have a cleaning staff to do that."

That did it. She slammed the mugs down on the granite counter, getting satisfaction from the sound. "I let most of the house and grounds staff go six months ago, when the accountant began talking about my dwindling funds."

His face reflected surprise. And that gave her satisfaction, too. When had she become so mean-spirited? When had she changed from a grieving widow who would have done anything to have her husband back again? When had she become this bitter shrew?

It was a silly question. The answer was easy—horrifyingly easy.

This morning. That's when. Around 2:00 a.m., when she'd come face-to-face with her dead husband.

"Irina, I'm sorry. I didn't expect the insurance company to drag out the investigation of my death. I guess I should have." He rubbed his palm across his cheek. "I know all this has been hard on you."

"Hard on me?" she squeaked. "Hard—? Yes. You could say it's been hard."

She neatly and carefully folded the dish towel and laid it on the counter, using the mundane movements to gather her composure.

"Is everyone else gone?" She tried her best to keep her tone conversational.

"Yeah. Dan Taylor went—wherever he goes. Matt went to the guesthouse, where he's staying with Aimee and her son. And Deke went back to the hospital.

"Oh, Mindy. How is she? I didn't get a chance to ask Deke."

"No, you were too busy making coffee and washing dishes."

"Do not—"

"Sorry. He said they've gotten her blood sugar back to normal, but they're keeping her there for observation. At least that's what she thinks. Deke has made arrangements with the hospital director to keep her there in a protective custody situation until he's comfortable that she's no longer in danger."

"Tangled webs," she muttered on a sigh. Exhaustion shrouded her.

"What?" he snapped.

She shook her head. She felt so tired. Bone weary, as she'd heard Brock say many times. She'd only had about two hours of sleep last night before the dream woke her. Two hours in thirty-six.

"Never mind. I heard you. You said 'tangled webs.' Is that what you think I've done? You think I caused all this?"

"I think all of this is here because of your decision to fake your death. I think your arrogance has ruined many lives. Not only mine, but all these other people who care about you and are loyal to you."

He grimaced and shook his head. "I had to do it."

"No, you didn't. That is the arrogance. You decided you were the only person in the world who could stop Novus Ordo. And you had to do it alone." She flipped off the light switch.

The room plunged into darkness, startling her. She hadn't realized that Rook had turned off the conference room lights. The only relief from total darkness was the glow of a couple of night-lights.

Lifting her chin, she stepped toward the door, but Rook didn't step aside, as she'd expected him to. So she nearly collided with him.

"Excuse me," she said coldly.

"No."

She was way too close to him. Close enough that she could smell his fresh clean scent. She held her breath.

"Ex-cuse me," she repeated.

"No." He ran his palm down her upper arm. "We need to talk. *I* need to talk, and you need to listen."

His hand was as strong and warm as she remembered. She stiffened even more and took a small step backward.

"Don't do this," she said evenly. "I will listen to you. But not tonight—today, I mean. You've been gone for two years. *Dead* for two years. I am sure one more day can't make that much difference."

He held on to her for a few seconds, his head bent enough that he could look into her eyes. He wanted her to look at him. To yield to him.

She wouldn't. She couldn't. Not now. She had no idea what she was going to do, now that Rook was back. Yesterday he was dead. Today he was alive.

Until she could process everything that had happened in the past few hours, never mind the past two weeks or two years, she couldn't afford to allow herself to relax. She had to maintain control.

Control was all she had left.

"That's not true," he murmured.

For an instant she thought he'd read her mind. Then he continued.

"One day *can* make all the difference. The most dangerous man in the world wants me dead, and he'll do anything—*anything*—to make it happen. That includes killing you."

His hand tightened for an instant, maybe with emotion? She didn't dare believe that. But she had to believe what he said. Her life was in danger, and apparently her safety was in his hands—the same hands that had held her heart and then broken it.

"All right. I'll listen."

She heard his breath escape in a sigh. His hand slid from her arm to the small of her back. "Let me reset the access code and we can go up to our—to your suite."

Just what she didn't want to happen. She'd almost gotten rid of his scent. And now he was going to stamp it on everything again. The bathroom, the bed linens. Her.

They rode upstairs in the elevator that was disguised as a closet in the executive offices upstairs.

Rook paused at the elevator door as he took in the changes she'd made to his masculine office in the past two years. She watched him as his gaze lit on vases and fresh flowers and candles, the new, colorful cushions that brightened the dark wood and tan walls, and the airy curtains on the wide windows that he'd always wanted bare.

He took a deep breath and his nose wrinkled, and she knew he'd noticed the subtle smell of fresh flowers and scented candles.

"Nice," he said, that edge of sarcasm tingeing his voice.

She could have predicted his reaction. He'd indulged her liking for beautiful feminine things, but reluctantly, in typical male fashion. It was one of the things they'd bantered intimately about. One of the things she'd missed so much.

"Don't," she snapped.

"Don't what?"

"Don't tease me as if nothing has changed. I had to do something. Your—your ghost in this house haunted me."

"So you had me exorcised with aromatherapy?"

Hurt arrowed through her. "This is not a joke. Maybe it was easy for you to wipe me out of your mind. You didn't have to live here, surrounded by *my* clothes, *my* scent, *my* ghost in every room."

He looked at her, and for an instant the veneer of

command and confidence that he carried with him fell away, and raw anguish etched new lines in his face. But the instant passed, as if it had never been.

He turned to stare out the picture window and ran a finger across the large mahogany desk. "Do you want to talk in your suite?" he asked.

Her immediate reaction was to say no. All her bravado about wiping his presence out of the house was a shield she'd thrown up to protect her vulnerable emotions. He would see through her as soon as he stepped into their bedroom. She'd made changes to the open areas of the ranch house, but their bedroom was the same as it had always been.

She'd been trying to convince herself that it was time to let him go. That two years of sleeping with his ghost was long enough. And she'd almost succeeded.

"That's okay," he added. "We can talk here. Hopefully no one will interrupt us. And I don't want to make things awkward for you."

Too late for that.

He looked past her. "Are the rooms across the hall from the suite empty?"

Suddenly, and inexplicably, Irina wanted to cry. Was he trying to spare her, or himself?

"No," she said. "I mean, yes, they're empty, but you have no need to do that. It's probably best if we keep a low profile." She uttered a small laugh. "Awkward would be if everyone knew we were sleeping in separate rooms."

"Fine. I'll sleep on the sofa." He sent her a look. "The sofa's still there, right? I mean—have you changed the bedroom?"

"Of course not." Unable to look at him, she headed out the door and down the hall to the east wing. Rook's shoes echoed on the hardwood floors behind her.

He was her husband, and he was back from the dead. So why did she feel like she was on her way to the guillotine?

BY THE TIME IRINA had finished her shower and come out of her dressing room, Rook had fallen asleep on the sofa that sat opposite the king-size bed.

She studied him closely. Was he pretending, in order to avoid the questions he knew she was going to ask?

No. He really was asleep. A glow of sunlight creeping around the edges of the drapes illuminated his face. His strong, even features were soft and relaxed, something that never happened while he was awake. Still, even in sleep, the lines she'd noticed earlier were still there, scoring the corners of his mouth. Lines that hadn't been there two years before.

She wanted to trace them with her fingertips. Wipe them away. Why were they there? Pain? Fatigue? Worry?

All of the above?

She was surprised and a little hurt that he could sleep.

She hadn't slept for two years. Every time she closed her eyes, she dreamed that dream. He was with her, in her, loving her, and then he was gone, sinking into the dark waters of the Mediterranean.

Her feelings were in turmoil. A part of her felt comforted by his presence, but at the same time, her limbs were rigid with trepidation, as if she were alone in a room with a sinister stranger.

Not surprising. In a way, that's exactly what he was. A stranger.

She wrapped the terry-cloth robe more tightly around her and lay down on her side, still watching him sleep.

After a few moments, her vision blurred and her eyelids prickled. She touched the corner of her eye and was surprised to feel a warm wetness.

She was crying. She who never cried. Hadn't for years. She blinked rapidly. There was nothing to cry about now. Rook was back. He was alive.

Nothing in her life could measure up to the joy of discovering that the man whom she'd loved from the first moment she'd laid eyes on him was alive.

However, nothing could measure up to the enormity of his betrayal, either. He'd let her believe he was dead.

She pressed her lips together as a sob gathered in her throat. It was too much to bear. To lose him only to find out that he'd lied to her—lied to everyone. He'd left her alone.

And he'd done it deliberately.

She thought back on the days, the weeks, prior to his death. He said he'd been planning it for months. When had he changed? Was there a moment that she could pinpoint as different?

She didn't know. All she knew was that the strong, dependable protector who had rescued her father and her from the wrath of the former Soviet Union, and the sweet, attentive lover who'd wooed her during the following months, then asked her to marry him, had somehow slipped away without her noticing.

By the time her father died, a year later, Rook was well on his way to becoming the soldier who'd appeared before her in the cabin, his olive-green eyes cold and opaque as jade, his demeanor more like a newly extracted deep-op than a returning lover.

She tried to think about her first glimpse of him in the cabin, his body lit by firelight and obscured by shadow. It had been several moments before she saw his face. He'd had plenty of time to mask his feelings.

What had he thought when he'd seen her for the first time in two years? Had his gaze turned soft as emerald velvet like it had when they'd first become lovers? Or had it been distorted by the raw pain she'd glimpsed when she'd accused him of wiping her out of his mind?

He stirred, startling her. His brows twitched and lowered, his chest rose and fell rapidly. He tossed his head and arched his back, as if gulping for air.

Irina sat up quietly. Rook had never had nightmares. She could only remember being awakened by him one time. It was a few months after he'd returned from rescuing Travis Ronson.

He'd cried out in his sleep but had quieted immediately when she touched his forehead. The next morning he hadn't remembered anything about it.

She glided over the hardwood floor without making a sound and crouched beside the couch. This close, she could see sweat glistening on his forehead and neck.

Maybe he was sick. Hesitantly, she reached out a hand. Her fingertips brushed his forehead.

His eyes flew open, and in one motion he threw back the blanket and pointed a big gun directly at her forehead.

She scrambled away but lost her balance and ended up on her butt. Horrified, she scooted backward across the floor.

The next few seconds stretched out in slow motion. Rook's eyes went from glazed with sleep to sharp and clear as green bottle glass. His knuckles turned white around his gun. His finger tightened on the trigger.

A subsonic rhythmic roar filled her ears.

Finally, he lowered the weapon. He stared at her,

blinked, stared again and then looked down at his hands.

Once he broke eye contact, time returned to normal. But that was the only thing that did. Her heart still pounded like a jackhammer, stealing her breath. Her arms and legs were rigid with tension. And her brain was spinning too fast to settle on a single coherent thought.

Her husband's shocked face filled her vision.

"What are you doing?" he gasped.

She held up shaking hands, palms out. "H-hoping you are not going to shoot me."

He eyed the gun as if it were a rat or a spider. Then he set it down on the arm of the sofa and sat up, pushing his fingers through his hair. "Go back to bed."

"Rook—"

"Just go. I won't bother you anymore. I'll sleep across the hall."

"No."

His head jerked up.

"This cannot continue, Rook. You told me you needed me to listen. Well, I am here. I am listening. I deserve explanations, answers." It was a struggle to speak evenly. Her throat closed up.

He lowered his forearms to his knees and leaned forward, his head down. "Yes, you do."

Her scalp tingled with relief. She picked herself up off the floor and sat on the edge of a slipper chair across from the sofa.

For a few seconds, Rook sat there, his head in his hands. Then he rubbed his eyes and his chin and stood.

For the first time, she noticed that he was dressed in nothing but dark dress pants. The belt was undone and the too-big pants hung low on his hips.

He'd always been lean, with long straps of muscles that rippled under his golden skin. But he'd lost at least twenty pounds in the past two years, so his body, which had always been buff and muscular, was now wiry.

Her gaze came to rest on a vaguely circular scar on his upper right chest. "Oh," she whispered.

Rook knew what she was looking at. His hand twitched to cover the scar—the place where Deke's bullet had entered his chest.

He still remembered the hot rush of panic as the slug impacted him. The instant of horror and regret. In all his planning, he'd never once thought about how the bullet would feel. He'd given Deke specific instructions to aim for his right upper chest. But until the instant of impact, he hadn't seriously considered that the shot might be fatal.

The self-consciousness he suddenly felt about his body heightened his awareness of hers.

She had on a white terry-cloth robe, belted at the waist. It gaped open at the top and the bottom, revealing the curves and cleavage of her delicately rounded breasts and a glimpse of her thighs. She was decently covered, but her perfect body made the robe seem X-rated.

She'd lost weight during the two years he'd been gone, which meant she wasn't quite as curvy as she had been. Her hips didn't swell out from her slender waist like they once had. Her breasts weren't as full and plump. But she was as beautiful and desirable as she'd ever been.

More so. After all, he'd been alone for two years.

And so had she.

He forced his gaze away from her beautiful breasts. When he met her eyes, the awareness he felt flared like a flame. But too soon, her gaze wavered, reminding him that he had no right. Not anymore.

"What do you want to know?" he asked flatly.

Chapter Eight

Irina stared at Rook as his question echoed in her ears. *What do you want to know?*

He looked back at her, his face carefully wiped clean of any emotion, his body still—unnaturally so, even for him. He'd always radiated a calm command that put people at ease.

This was different. He looked as though he were facing a firing squad.

She shook her head, resenting the fact that he was turning it back onto her. He'd said he wanted her to listen. Now he was demanding that she figure out what questions to ask.

"I want to know everything," she said, spreading her hands, palms out. "Where have you been? What have you been doing? How did you plan this for months and never once let anything slip?"

His gaze didn't waver, but his chin lifted a fraction and he swallowed. He wasn't as calm as she'd thought.

"How—how could you leave me?"

Then his gaze did waver.

"I thought I had everything planned," he said. "I didn't realize how hard it was going to be, to be shot. To swim. To survive."

Irina didn't speak.

"I attached a wetsuit, diving gear and two air tanks to the bottom of the boat before we set out. But when I hit the water after Deke shot me, it knocked me unconscious for a few seconds. I thought I was dead. When I realized I wasn't—" he shook his head "—I was disappointed."

"You *wanted* to die?" she burst out.

He shrugged. "I thought it was the only way I could keep you safe."

The words from her nightmare. She shook her head. "No. I don't believe you."

"I managed to wake up before I drowned. I found the air tanks and gear, but I couldn't get the wetsuit on. The Mediterranean is damned cold. I swam for probably two miles, floating with the currents as much as possible. By the time I got out of the water I was hypothermic and I'd lost a lot of blood." His voice sounded strained. He sat down on the couch.

"I'd stashed local currency with the diving gear, so I ditched the gear, found an isolated farmhouse and pretended I had amnesia. I gave the farmer a lot of money to keep quiet about helping me."

Irina hunched her shoulders and crossed her arms. Who was he? This man who'd planned such an intricate deception? And how pathetic was she that she'd never suspected a thing?

"Where were you all this time?" She had to fight to keep her tone even.

"For six months I was with the family. I set up a trust for them through the Cayman account. Then I made my way across Europe and Asia to Mahjidastan. I'd been there about three months when Deke called."

"You were there, in the same place as Matt, for three months?"

"Mahjidastan is a tiny province, but I was doing my best not to be noticed. I'm sure Matt was, too. I had no idea you were searching for me until I got that message from Deke."

"If you wanted that terrorist to think you were dead, why did you go there? Is that not where the U.S. thinks he is?"

"That's one of the reasons I did it—to find him. To try and stop him."

"Was it worth it?"

Rook blinked. She'd gotten to him with that question. He opened his mouth, then closed it again. Then he lay back down on the sofa and threw an arm over his eyes.

"I don't know, Irina," he muttered. "I really don't know.

ROOK GASPED and clutched at his chest. It was wet. He checked his hand. *No blood.* Sweat, but no blood. Relief stung his eyes.

It was a dream. *The* dream. He wasn't bleeding— or drowning. He sat up and put his bare feet on the floor, and froze. The floor wasn't grimy, cracked vinyl with sand in all the crevices. It was warm, smooth wood. Polished, new, expensive.

He lifted his head and took a deep breath. The scent of gardenias filled his senses, a far cry from the smell of dust and sweat and heat.

He wasn't in Mahjidastan. He rubbed his eyes and looked around. The pale pink night-light played tricks on his eyes, just as the after-effects of his dream played tricks on his brain.

Irina. He was in Irina's bedroom. They'd argued and he'd fallen asleep on the sofa. Squinting at the king-size bed, he made out her gently curved form. She was lying on her side, with her back to him. She was still asleep—so far.

He made his way carefully into the dressing room and slid the pocket doors closed before he turned on the light.

He turned on the hot water and ran his hands under the flow. He'd forgotten the feel of clean, fresh, hot water. The best he'd gotten in Mahjidastan was a trickle of lukewarm brownish liquid. He splashed his face again and again, until the water got too hot to bear. Then he turned it off and started on the cold water.

After dousing his face with a few double handfuls, he cupped his hands and rinsed his mouth with the cold, delicious liquid. Then he leaned his forearms on the edge of the ceramic sink and waited for the nausea and panic to pass. A couple of deep breaths slowed his racing pulse.

He'd hoped he was done with the dream, now that he was back home—back from the dead. It was always the same—the sharp blow to his upper chest, the spasm of fear and regret as his arms and legs collapsed.

Irina's anguished screams—her fingers grasping at his arm, his shirt, his hair. But inevitably she couldn't hold on and he tumbled overboard into the dark waters of the Mediterranean.

The last thing he saw was her face distorted by water and the sun's brilliant glare.

He grabbed a towel and swiped it over his neck and chest, and then his face. The soft Egyptian cotton soaked up the water but didn't wipe away the dream.

He peered in the mirror—and stared. He still wasn't used to seeing his bare face. He still expected unkempt, untrimmed hair and beard—a simple disguise in a barren East Asian mountain village. Although he'd long ago accepted the bearded face. This clean-shaven face and neatly trimmed hair seemed more like a mask. Was not recognizing one's own face the measure of a good disguise?

With a nearly silent groan, he arched his sore shoulders and neck. The day before had been a long one. And today would probably be longer.

He ran his damp fingers through his hair and straightened, arching his aching neck.

He took a deep breath, wiped a dribble of water from his cheek and hiked up his pants from where they'd ridden down over the waistband of his briefs.

Instinctively, he reached around to the small of his back to check his paddle holster. But it wasn't there. The holster and his Sig Sauer were lying on the sofa.

He winced. He should have been more careful. Her terror-filled eyes had pierced his heart. He wished he could explain why he felt he had to sleep with a weapon, even here, even in her room. But she wouldn't understand.

He didn't want her to understand. She'd always hated guns. Her childhood had been permeated with guns and bombs. She'd grown up in the collapsing former Soviet Union, with its chaos and civil wars.

When he'd rescued her and her father, when he'd fallen in love with her, he'd promised her she'd never have to live in fear again. And he'd broken that promise. That one and many others.

A quiet knock at the pocket doors startled him. He opened them. Irina was standing there, in a sleek nightgown the color of candlelight. It was sleeveless and long. The material was opaque and draped across her breasts and waist and hips like wavelets in a shallow pool.

Her blond hair shimmered brightly against her pale shoulders, and her blue eyes were dark with worry.

"Rook? Are you all right?"

"Yeah, sorry. I didn't mean to wake you." He tried not to look at her, but his eyes refused to obey his brain.

"You—called out my name."

"It was just a dream," he said, rubbing the back of his neck nervously. "It's over now." He pushed past her, and his bare arm brushed against her breast.

She uttered a tiny gasp.

He clenched his jaw, determined to walk on by her, back to the sofa. But try as he might, he couldn't take another step.

He turned toward her, willing her to do what he couldn't. All she had to do was take one step backward. One small step, and he'd know she was rejecting him.

But she didn't move, unless leaning forward was considered moving.

He lowered his head. She raised hers. Their lips touched for the first time in two years.

Both of them jerked away, startled by the electricity that sparked between them.

Her gaze flickered, and he was sure she would stop, but then her eyelids drifted shut and she raised her head a fraction more.

He kissed her, deeply, fully, drinking in the feel of her mouth beneath his. Those full lips soft and trembling, her small sweet tongue, her breath.

Time swirled around them, meaningless. It had been two years, but it could have been yesterday.

Irina couldn't breathe, but she didn't care. Rook was breathing for her. He was feeding her life and breath through his kisses. Without his mouth on hers, she knew she would die.

He lifted his hands and cradled her face, as he deepened the kiss even more. She had a vague impression

Play the Lucky Hearts Game

and get...

2 FREE BOOKS and
2 FREE Mystery GIFTS...
YOURS to KEEP!

Yes! I have scratched off the gold card. Please send me my *2 FREE BOOKS* and *2 FREE Mystery GIFTS* (gifts are worth about $10). I understand that I am under no obligation to purchase any books as explained on the back of this card.

Scratch Here!
Then look below to see what your cards get you...2 Free Books & 2 Free Mystery Gifts!

We want to make sure we offer you the best service suited to your needs. Please answer the following question:

About how many NEW paperback fiction books have you purchased in the past 3 months?
❏ 0-2   ❏ 3-6   ❏ 7 or more

❏ I prefer the regular-print edition   ❏ I prefer the larger-print edition
382 HDL EZXK   182 HDL EZJW   399 HDL EZXV   199 HDL EZJ9

FIRST NAME   LAST NAME

ADDRESS

APT.   CITY

Visit us online at
www.ReaderService.com

STATE / PROV.   ZIP/POSTAL CODE

Twenty-one gets you
2 FREE BOOKS and
2 FREE MYSTERY GIFTS!

Twenty gets you
2 FREE BOOKS!

Nineteen gets you
1 FREE BOOK!

TRY AGAIN!

The Reader Service—Here's how it works:

BUSINESS REPLY MAIL
FIRST-CLASS MAIL   PERMIT NO. 717   BUFFALO, NY

POSTAGE WILL BE PAID BY ADDRESSEE

THE READER SERVICE
PO BOX 1867
BUFFALO NY 14240-9952

NO POSTAGE
NECESSARY
IF MAILED
IN THE
UNITED STATES

that his hands were rougher, more callused than she remembered them. As soon as that thought hit her brain, it was gone, lost in sensation.

He slid his hands down to her shoulders, her back, her waist. She leaned into him, pressing her breasts against his bare chest. Her nipples were tight and distended, almost painfully sensitized. When they brushed against his skin, a deep, erotic thrill surged through her, weakening her knees and stealing her breath.

She was sure nothing could surpass the feeling of his mouth on hers, his chest against her breasts, the heat of his hands caressing her body. But he slid his hand further, from her waist to her rounded bottom, and pressed her to him, until the searing heat of his erection branded her skin.

He lifted his head and took a ragged breath. His eyes were soft, questioning. His erection pulsed against her, leaving no doubt what he wanted.

She nodded and pressed her lips against his collarbone.

"Rina..."

"Yes," she whispered.

He lifted her and laid her on the bed. With a conciseness of movement, he was in her. She gasped and arched her back as she felt the familiar, unbearably erotic sensation of being filled by him.

"Oh, Rook," she breathed. "I've missed you so much."

He stopped her words with his mouth as he pushed deeper.

Irina couldn't control herself, and it was obvious Rook was having the same problem. He thrust deeply, desperately, sending her to the apex of sensation within seconds. He stopped and pressed his face into the curve of her shoulder, breathing harshly.

She pushed her fingers through his hair.

The phone rang.

She jumped as the shrill noise cut through her erotic haze, and pushed at his chest.

He rolled away.

She crawled across around the bed and picked up the handset. "Yes?" she said coldly.

"Mrs. Castle, this is Dan Taylor. I apologize for bothering you, but I need to speak to Colonel Castle."

Irina held out the handset without looking at him. "It's for you."

Rook took the phone from her hand. "Castle," he said shortly.

Irina got up and folded her arms across her revealing nightgown. She felt naked and exposed.

Rook rubbed his temples as he listened. Then he shook his head and muttered a curse. "When?"

The tone of his voice told her something had happened.

"Where are you? Where is he? I'll be right there." He hung up and turned.

"I have to go," he said, his voice tense and carefully even. He started toward the door, adjusting his pants and picking up his shirt along the way.

"What's wrong?"

He turned back to send her a warning look. "I've got to get out of here. I'll wash up across the hall. You stay here. Lock the door and don't open it for anyone but me. Brock's been shot."

FIVE MINUTES LATER, Rook headed downstairs. A long, shaky breath escaped his lips. Dan's phone call had interrupted something that shouldn't have ever happened.

He'd known the instant he laid eyes on Irina that if

he touched her, he'd be lost. He'd told himself a hundred times that he had no right.

But, dear God, he'd missed her. He'd missed that mouth, that body. He'd missed the way she opened to him, welcomed him. He'd missed being her lover.

He knew by the look in her eyes as he'd closed the suite's door that she felt abandoned.

But Brock O'Neill, the man he trusted most after his oath brothers, had been injured, and no matter what his personal feelings, he had a responsibility.

He headed through the house and out the front door. Immediately, he saw Dan Taylor standing beside the open passenger door of an idling black SUV. Taylor spotted him and climbed in. The SUV pulled up beside Rook and he got into the backseat.

"What happened? Did you catch the shooter?"

"I don't have specifics. Captain O'Neill notified one of my men via push-to-talk."

"What was Brock doing on that ridge?"

"Lieutenant Parker suggested a few days ago that the specialists patrol the perimeter, just to be sure that the remote areas of the ranch weren't breached."

Taylor continued to fill Rook in as he drove to the ridge. "I called and dispatched Major Hathaway over there immediately, since she has medical expertise, and sent two agents to meet her. Then I called you."

"Fiona's here at the ranch?"

Dan nodded. "I assumed you knew. She came in earlier this afternoon, according to my gate guard." He paused for an instant. "Timely."

The single word held a wealth of meaning. Rook sent him a sidelong glance. "You've added her to your suspect list."

"Just making a comment."

As soon as he got out of the car, Rook saw Fiona and Brock. Brock was sitting in the open door of an SUV, and Fiona was taping his upper arm.

"Fee, Brock," he called as he sprinted over.

They looked up. Brock's usually impassive face held a sheepish expression.

"Rook!" Fiona gasped, as the roll of gauze dropped from her fingers. Her hands covered her mouth. "Oh, my God. Brock told me, but—" she shook her head "—I can't believe you're here. You're— Oh, my God."

"Don't faint on me, Fee," he said gently. "It's good to see you."

"Oh, my!" She threw her arms around him and hugged him, then pushed back to look at him again. "It is great to see you! I don't know what to say."

"Just hearing that you're glad to see me is enough."

He met Brock's gaze. "Didn't take you long to get into trouble."

Brock's sheepish expression etched more deeply into his face. "Never does," he said wryly.

"What happened?"

"I was out patrolling. I caught a glint of light on metal and came over to investigate. It was a booby trap." He looked at his upper arm in disgust.

"A booby trap?" Rook repeated. "How in hell—"

"Hold still," Fiona snapped at Brock. She'd unwrapped the roll of gauze and was positioning it over the bandages.

She spoke to Rook without taking her eyes off her handiwork. "The bullet went through the meaty part of his biceps. I've sterilized the wound and I'm wrapping it. It missed the humerus, or it would have shattered. He's lucky he's still got his arm."

"I'll tell you who's lucky," Brock growled. "Whoever rigged that rifle. But his luck's going to run out once I catch up with him."

"Stop fidgeting," Fiona snapped, as she wound the gauze around one last time and taped it. "Let's get you to the emergency room."

"No. We don't have time for that nonsense," Brock growled. "Rook, I want to examine the area before those guys stomp all over it."

Rook looked at Fiona, who raised a perfectly shaped brow. She wanted Brock's arm looked at by a physician. "We'll try to keep it clean for you."

As he rose, he caught the victorious glare Fiona threw at Brock.

"Taylor, can you spare a man to take Captain O'Neill to the ER? Fiona, go with them."

Taylor nodded and gestured to one of his men.

"Now, where's the booby trap?"

"Over here, sir," one of Taylor's agents called. "It's a pretty simple setup. The brilliant part is the placement."

Rook saw what he meant. The trip wire was placed so that anyone getting close enough to trip it would be dead in line with the barrel. The weapon used was simple—a .22 with a silencer, very reliable and very deadly at close range. It was a miracle that Brock wasn't dead.

Actually, he amended to himself, it was a testament to Brock's uncanny awareness of everything around him and his lightning-fast reflexes.

Rook looked around. From where he was standing he could see the front of the ranch house and the roofs of the guesthouses. A high-powered sniper rifle in the right hands could pick off anyone.

"And take a look at this," the agent said. "The rifle's

trigger mechanism is hooked up to a cell phone, probably prepaid."

"A cell phone?"

"Yes, sir. It was rigged to call a number, almost certainly another prepaid cell. Someone was notified that the trap had been tripped."

"Can you trace that phone? Find out where it was bought? Or trace the numbers by area code?"

Taylor walked over. "We'll do what we can, but it's pretty unlikely. If they have any sense at all, they wouldn't have bought them anywhere near here. Besides, you can get all the anonymous phones you want over the Internet."

He glanced over his shoulder at the ranch house. "What's the point of a booby trap? It just calls attention to itself."

"Hang on a minute, Fee." Brock's voice came from behind them. He walked over to stand by Dan. "We were taking shifts patrolling the perimeter. My guess is—" he swept his uninjured arm through the air "—they were planning to set up a sniper's nest up here. Think about it. They already tried to pick off Rafe and Aaron in the hospital parking lot. I'm guessing the trap was set up to kill anyone who found it, and the cell phone notified them to come remove the rifle and the triggers before anyone found the body."

"So the plan was that whoever got too close would die, and they could swoop in, grab the evidence, maybe even the body, and get out. Sounds like they didn't expect you to outrun the bullet," Rook commented.

Brock's lip curled up. "I lost an eye, but I've still got two good ears. I heard the wire sing just before it tripped."

Rook clapped his friend on the back. "Glad your hearing works. Now get to the hospital and get patched up."

Dan stepped over to Rook's side and held out his hand to Fiona, who was putting away her first-aid kit. "Major Hathaway? I'm Special Agent Dan Taylor, with the Secret Service."

She took his hand. "Special Agent Taylor. Glad to meet you."

"My agents told me you'd arrived. I understand you have a newborn baby."

Rook met Brock's gaze and both of them winced.

"Is my child a part of your investigation, Special Agent Taylor?"

Dan's cheeks brightened. "No, ma'am. Of course not. I—"

"Then I fail to see the pertinence of your statement."

"Fee," Rook broke in. "Make sure that Brock rests for a while when he gets back. Now you two need to get going."

Fiona's golden brown eyes shot daggers at the Secret Service agent, but she nodded. "Come on, Brock. Get in the car like a good boy."

Then she turned back to Rook. "I don't think I've ever been more glad to see anyone, but I hope for Irina's sake that you had amnesia or something. She's been shattered without you."

He nodded, not meeting her gaze.

As the SUV pulled away, Rook studied the view of the ranch buildings below and then assessed the ridge. He walked back and forth, measuring with his eyes.

"Sir?"

He held up a hand, still concentrating, then he saw it.

"Here." He stood back, squinting, then stepped over to the suspicious-looking area. Leaves had been scattered artlessly over the flat ground.

"Take a look."

Dan followed his gaze. "What am I looking at?"

"That blanket of leaves. That tree limb. Take a closer look. I'll bet the smallest branches have been cut or broken off."

"You think it's—"

"The sniper's nest. He hides behind the limb and uses it as a brace for his rifle. Another two minutes and Brock would have seen it." Rook crouched and looked downhill. "I don't want to disturb any evidence, but I'm betting that if you sight just above the level of that fallen branch, you'll see the front door of the ranch house."

Rook bent down and sighted along the trajectory. "This is very well done. Well thought out. Hidden in plain sight. I agree with you about the booby trap. Why did they bother? Why not just leave this as is? Very few people would figure out at a glance what it is."

"Hey, Dan," one of the agents called out. "Come take a look at this." He was standing a few feet behind the booby trap.

Dan walked over. Rook followed him. The agent hadn't moved. He pointed.

Rook saw another blanket of leaves, thicker than the sniper's nest.

"What is it, Ferrell?" Dan asked.

"See that? Under the edge of that bush?"

Then Rook spotted it. "Something metallic. Right there."

"I didn't want to disturb anything until you'd seen it," Ferrell said.

"Check it out, but be careful. If that's what I think it is, this area could be booby-trapped, too."

Ferrell worked carefully and smoothly. After a minute, Rook could see that the hidden piece of metal was a sniper rifle. After Ferrell uncovered the rifle, he dug out a pair of high-powered binoculars from underneath.

"Okay, so this is the reason for the booby trap, I take it," Rook commented. "But still, the hiding place was good enough to fool anyone who wasn't combing the area." He propped his fists on his hips. "Now I have two questions. Why booby-trap a hiding place this good? And for that matter, why leave the equipment here at all? Seems as if these guys were begging to be caught."

Another agent came hiking up the ridge from behind them. "Dan, we've found the breach in the fence where they got in. It's a tiny break, back that way."

"That's an old farm road back in there," Rook said. "Hardly used anymore."

Dan nodded. "Probably exactly why they chose it. I'm guessing they didn't want to haul the equipment in each time they came, in case they were spotted."

Rook nodded. "Carrying a super-long-range rifle and state-of-the-art binoculars wouldn't be easy to explain. Without them, they could say they were lost and looking for someone to help them." He straightened.

"Get Deke over here to take a look at this. I'm not familiar with that model, but he knows all of them. He might even be able to give you a short list of shooters. There aren't many who are good enough to make a shot this long."

Dan nodded. "Ferrell, get the kits. See if you can lift any fingerprints or shoe prints."

Rook walked back over to the sniper's nest with Dan beside him. "Get Deke and Brock to look at this, too. Brock can give you a good estimate of the height and weight of the sniper, and Deke just might know him. And listen. I'd like for you to hold off disturbing the scene until Brock has a chance to go over the area. If there's any trace here, he'll find it."

"Sir, I have a crime scene expert on my team."

"A good one, I'm sure. How much experience?"

Dan took a long breath. "Five years."

"Impressive. Brock O'Neill has been tracking and hunting in these mountains since he was old enough to walk. So he has thirty years' experience."

"All due respect, sir, O'Neill is still a suspect—"

Rook leveled a gaze at the young Secret Service agent that had silenced four-star generals. "Fiona will have Brock back here within a half hour. Use him. You and your expert will learn a lot."

The sound of boots crunching unevenly on grass and twigs caught Rook's ears.

He whirled, pulling his gun. At the same time, Dan and three of his agents did the same.

"Whoa. It's just me." It was Rafe Jackson. He spread his hands. He couldn't exactly hold them up because of his crutches.

Dan lowered his weapon and sent his men a quick nod. "Mr. Jackson, what are you doing here?" he asked. "Everyone was ordered to stay in their quarters."

Jackson smiled. "I didn't get that message. Sorry. I saw the activity up here and thought I'd investigate." He gestured with his head. "If I'd realized how steep that grade is—" He stopped, craning his neck. "Is that a rifle over there? Was someone hurt?"

Dan shifted slightly, just enough that Jackson would have to move to see beyond him.

Rook holstered his weapon and crossed his arms. "Special Agent Taylor asked you a question. What are you doing up here?"

Jackson's eyes narrowed and his jaw muscle flexed.

"I saw the activity and was curious about what was going on."

"Saw the activity from where?"

"Down there. The guest quarters."

Rook looked down. From his vantage point so close to the booby trap, all he could see was the roof of the guest quarters.

"Mr. Jackson," Dan said. "An agent will escort you back to the guesthouse. I hope it won't be a problem if we search your rooms. We'll be searching the entire guest quarters."

Jackson's gaze wavered then. "Search? If you'll tell me what you're looking for—" He stopped and laughed wryly. "Strike that. Of course, Agent Taylor. No problem whatsoever."

He planted his crutches and turned. A slight grimace marred his face, but he recovered immediately. "G'day, Colonel Castle."

Rook nodded.

Dan stood beside Rook, not speaking, until the agent and Jackson had started back down the hill.

"His leg is hurting. You could have had the agent drive him," Rook commented.

"I know," Taylor replied. "What do you think about him?"

"Hard to say."

"Nice for them, if they have someone on the inside that could check on their booby trap."

"What will be nice is if we can prove it."

Chapter Nine

After informing the agents that Brock and Deke would be handling the preliminary examination of the sniper's nest and booby trap, Dan and Rook headed into town. They left the ranch via the driveway from the underground garage to avoid any reporters who might be hovering around the front gate.

On the way, Rook called Deke, finding him at the hospital, visiting Mindy and his baby, and told him about Brock, the booby trap and Rafiq Jackson.

"Sure," Deke said. "They got spotlights out there? I'll head out right now. You really think Jackson could be Novus's mole?"

"Right now he's looking pretty good for it," Rook replied. "See if you can see the site from the house. At the time he got up there, we hadn't turned on the spotlights yet. And see if anyone else noticed the 'activity' that Jackson noticed. I want to know what you think about the booby trap, too. Is it rigged to kill, or to just look like it could kill?"

"What does that mean? Are you thinking Brock could have set it up and then shot himself?"

"We can't afford to rule out anyone at this point.

Three of our four agents have been wounded. I'm making the assumption that we can eliminate Fiona, since she was having a baby when Irina called off her search and alerted Novus Ordo. That means if it's any of the other three, then they had to have taken a bullet on purpose. And I'm here to tell you, nobody does that without a lot of soul-searching." He swallowed. "I mean, would you rather be grazed at the temple by a long-range sniper shot, take a chance on bleeding out from your femoral artery or have confidence that you're fast enough to dodge a rifle shot at close range?"

Deke didn't say anything for a couple of seconds. "Or," he said slowly, "trust your best friend to shoot you in the chest without killing you?"

Rook was stunned by the emotion in Deke's voice. He knew he'd asked a lot of his friend, but it hadn't really hit him until now just how much. He'd essentially asked Deke to kill him.

And let him think he had. What kind of arrogant bastard was he, to do that to his best friend?

And his own wife.

"Deke, I—"

"I'll get back with you," Deke said quickly, and hung up.

Taylor pulled up in front of a nondescript government building in Sundance. A weathered sign out front identified it as a U.S. Treasury building. A smaller, dimly lit sign beside the front door read Census Bureau.

Rook nodded. "Good cover," he said.

Taylor nodded. "The Treasury guys moved to the downtown federal building several years ago. Secret Service took over this building when they arrived." He smiled. "Nobody bothers the Census Bureau. The first floor is mostly empty. A receptionist desk that's never manned. We've got locks on the elevators, so no one wandering in can get upstairs. Third floor has been converted into sleeping quarters for the agents."

He led Rook through the lobby and into an elevator. "We're holding the prisoners on the second floor. No one-way glass, but I do have monitors."

"What have you gotten out of them?"

"Nothing yet. They're acting like they don't understand English. I'm trying to locate a translator, but—"

Rook blew out a frustrated breath and shook his head.

Dan raised his brows. "Are you thinking about—"

"Jackson? He speaks the language," Rook replied. "We'd need to record and verify what he says, though."

"We can send the recording to Homeland Security's language lab, but I don't know what kind of lag time they're experiencing right now."

"Can't we claim executive order as a top priority? We're listening to people who are directly linked to the most murderous, most elusive terrorist on the planet."

"Colonel, I wish it were that easy." Taylor shook his head. "But at any one time Homeland Security is listening in on dozens of conversations from different sources, not to mention other agencies. Any one of those conversations could be a discussion of a plan to attack the U.S."

Rook knew Taylor was right, but it still chafed. "Let's do it. Let's bring him in to translate. You call your boss, and I'll put a call in to the Pentagon."

As they stepped out of the elevator on the second floor, Taylor pointed to a door several feet to the right. When he unlocked and opened the door, a man in a white T-shirt and blue jeans with a shoulder holster got up from a table where three monitors and three keyboards sat.

He picked up a half-eaten burger and tossed it in the trash. Then he picked up a cup of coffee.

"This is Special Agent Shawn Cutler. Shawn, this is Colonel Rook Castle."

"Pleasure, sir," Cutler said. They shook hands.

Rook sat down in front of the monitors. Two were trained on the two prisoners. One a wide-angle shot of the entire room, the other at a much closer angle. The third was a high, exterior view of the door.

"What's been going on, Shawn?"

"Not much. They're not talking. Not even to each other." He looked at the paper cup in his hand and shook his head. "This stuff is cold. I'm going to make some fresh. Can I bring you a cup?"

Rook shook his head. "Thanks, Shawn. I'm fine. Why don't you take a break while we're here."

Shawn nodded and left.

"I have two men posted outside that door," Taylor said. "As you see, the prisoners are stripped down to their underwear. They're handcuffed and hobbled. They've been thoroughly searched."

Rook grimaced at the tactics necessary for dealing with individuals who represented threats to national security. He understood that the safety of the nation and the free world was more important than the comfort and even dignity of a single criminal, but he didn't like it.

"Can you get me a closer look at their faces?"

"Sure." Taylor typed a few commands, and the monitor zoomed in.

Rook studied the men, who sat unmoving. One had his eyes closed. The other was staring at a spot on the table.

Rook shook his head. "It was a long shot. I hoped that in the flesh I might recognize one of them. But I'm sure I've never seen either of them before."

He sat back. "Where's the casualty? I want to see him, too."

"He's in the morgue at Crook County Medical Center. I don't advise going there, after all the business Black Hills Search and Rescue has given to the hospital in the past two weeks. There are already reporters waiting outside the gates at the ranch every day. If they find out you're alive, we won't be able to control them. In fact, we're lucky the networks haven't picked up on this yet."

"Good point," Rook said. "Okay. Let's get Jackson in here to question them. Are these monitors recording?"

"Not now. I can make them, though."

"Do it. Make sure you record Jackson's face, as well as the prisoners'. I'll get Matt to put together a word-for-word script for him to follow. We can send that in with the recording." Rook stood. "What about prints or DNA? Anything?"

"No ID on any of them. One had a push-to-talk, but we haven't found any others to connect it with. We're trying to trace it through the carrier. We've sent prints and DNA swabs, but I don't hold out much hope there. These guys are almost certainly here illegally."

"Okay then, what next?"

"I haven't had a chance to talk to you about Jackson, Gold and O'Neill. I questioned them individually after our meeting. Their stories seem to hold up, as far as they go. Not a one blinked. If one of them is the traitor, he has nerves of steel. If it's Jackson, I'd say more than just his *nerves* are made of steel, to come walking up to the booby trap like that."

"Right. It shocked him to see me, but he recovered quickly."

"For that matter, what about Brock? I agree with Deke. I think Brock is least likely to be the traitor. I've known him a long time, and I trust him almost as much as I trust Deke and Matt. But if it is him, then he walked right into the trap he set himself."

"Speaking of recordings, what about the meeting this morning. Do you have those disks ready?"

"Yeah. Haven't had a chance to go over them yet, though."

"I want to do that first thing in the morning. I want to study each specialist—see their reaction to the pictures of Ordo and Frank James. And then I want to call a meeting with everyone, talk about Brock's near miss and see what happens when I announce that they're all suspects."

"What about meeting here at 8:00 a.m.?"

"Okay, but let's get Deke and Brock over here by seven. I want to hear what they think about the sniper's nest before I face the other two. Get one of your agents to get them in here by 8:00 a.m. No, make it eight-thirty." He covered a yawn and continued. "Can we meet in your observation room?"

Dan nodded.

"When Aaron and Rafe come in, have those monitors running. Record them watching the prisoners. Unless I'm badly mistaken, one of them betrayed me."

Dan jotted some notes on his dog-eared notepad and then stood, looking at his watch. "I'll take care of all of that. It's after seven. This has been a long damn day. Even longer for you, I imagine."

Rook was taken aback. "Are you saying it's still Thursday?"

"I am. Why don't we got you away from here. Maybe take you to D.C., where we can protect you properly."

"No. I'm going back to the ranch. That's where my staff is—my family. Do what you have to do to keep us all safe there."

"Yes, sir. I suggest we get going then. I'm guessing you haven't slept since you got back to the States."

Rook thought about it. He actually couldn't remember the last time he'd really slept. The short nap earlier hardly counted, considering that he'd been dreaming he was in Mahjidastan when Irina had startled him awake.

Rook was prepared to spend the night in the guest suite. But when he got back to the ranch, he realized all his stuff was with Irina, in the suite that used to be theirs.

He unlocked the door as quietly as he could and slipped inside, easing it shut behind him. A pale nightlight kept the room from being totally dark.

When had she started sleeping with a night-light? His heart squeezed in his chest. He knew the answer to that question.

When he'd died.

He glanced around the shadowed room. There near the door to the dressing room was the battered fake-leather bag that he'd lived out of for the past two years. He picked it up and headed for the suite across the hall.

Just as his hand closed around the door handle, he heard her stir.

"Rook?" Her voice was soft and blurry with sleep. He closed his eyes, pushing away memories of her words, her touch, her taste, in the middle of the night.

"Just getting my bag," he said tightly.

"You should stay here."

"I need a shower, and I need to stretch out, get some rest. The sofa doesn't quite fit me."

"You don't have to sleep on the sofa. I mean, there's plenty of room here on the bed."

Her sleepy words awakened his body. He felt himself respond. Felt himself grow.

He clamped his jaw. His hand tightened on the door handle. He should refuse. If he stayed, he wouldn't get a wink of sleep.

With a sigh, he dropped his hand and turned around. "If you're sure," he said.

Her eyes glittered in the glow of the night-light. "Like I said earlier, it will avoid unnecessary awkwardness."

The sleepy sexiness was gone from her voice. Her tone was even. Her words crisp and clear. Their intent unmistakable.

I'm willing to do you this favor. Don't make any assumptions.

"Fine. I'll try not to disturb you."

She didn't say anything more. Rook heard the rustle of silk against satin as she lay back down.

For a few seconds he stood there, unmoving. Whether his senses were unnaturally heightened or whether his eyes had dark-adapted, he didn't know, but he could see her pale shoulders and arms against the paler sheets. He saw the undulating curves as her breasts rose and fell with her breaths. And he remembered, for the first time since the bullet slammed into his chest, how they felt—warm and firm and supple under his fingers.

Her body had always turned him on. It was perfect. The long, delicate bones, the generous breasts and buttocks, the tiny waist. And those legs that went on forever. She was so perfectly proportioned that she was almost a caricature of herself. A mockery of the perfect woman.

He ached with want, with need. His erection rubbed against the material of his briefs, ultra-sensitive. He didn't know what to do about it.

If he hadn't been dead in body for the past two years, he'd certainly been dead in soul. The long months stretched out behind him—an emotional black hole. He remembered nothing. No feelings of any kind, except a vague sense of emptiness, and an obsessive need to find Novus Ordo.

Now his body was reawakening, and lying beside her was going to be torture.

So he picked up his bag, went into the dressing room and turned on the water in the shower. After a second, he sighed and, with a small shudder, twisted the knob to cold.

IRINA TOOK A long breath and relaxed more deeply. She was deliciously warm, and she couldn't remember the last time she'd slept better. The familiar scent of soap and clean hair filled her nostrils. Smooth flesh, like silk over steel, was vibrant and warm under her fingertips.

How she loved waking up like this. Warm and safe and relaxed. She couldn't remember what day it was, and she had no sense of the time, but it didn't matter. It was night, and Rook was beside her.

She slid her fingers down from his chest to his flat stomach, and back up, feeling the ridge of breastbone under his warm skin. She turned her nose into the hollow of his shoulder and breathed deeply of the clean scent she could never get enough of.

Then she slid her fingers across his right nipple,

pausing to tease it until it hardened under the slight pressure she brought to bear on it.

He stirred, and she laughed softly. He'd never been quite comfortable when she played with his nipples. He wasn't sure if he was supposed to like it.

But she knew he did. She knew how sensitive— how erotically charged—they were. It turned him on when she touched them. She knew. Just like she knew that nibbling on his earlobe turned him on.

She knew because she knew his body.

With her eyes closed, she trailed her fingers across his pecs and up the side of his neck to his cheek, where she laid her open palm and pressed gently, turning his head toward her.

He turned slightly toward her, enough that she knew he was aroused, and splayed his hand over her tummy, then slid his palm upward and caressed the underside of her breasts.

He pressed his lips against her forehead and drew in a ragged breath. "Irina—"

A quiet whimper escaped from her throat. He'd said her name in his warning, longing voice. The voice that too often reminded her that he needed to get up and race to a meeting, or that she was late for an important charity event, or even just that he was too tired after some long, drawn-out mission.

"No," she whispered. "No protests. You do not protest. Not right now."

Something niggled at the edge of her brain, trying to interrupt her slow, lazy seduction of her husband. But she pushed it away. She'd woken up with a fiery need blazing deep within her, and *life,* with all its drudgery and problems and monkey wrenches, was not going to intrude, at least not until morning.

"Irina, it's—"

"I don't care what time it is, or what day. Right now you are under my spell." She lifted her head and sought his mouth, kissing him with languid, relaxed lips, darting her tongue in and out, teasing him the way she loved to do.

Rook Castle spent most of his life in a type A personality jet stream. She herself was focused, deliberate and slightly obsessive, but Rook was the poster child for type A.

Just about the only time he relaxed was when they were making love. And for some reason that she was too drowsy and too lazy to explore right now, it seemed particularly important to hold him with her in this erotic netherworld between sleeping and waking for as long as she could.

She nipped at his mouth with her teeth, then ran the tip of her tongue across his lips and down his chin to its soft underside. Just as she knew it would, his head lifted and his breath caught. Another erogenous zone she'd discovered.

Maybe today was the day to find a new one. She started on her quest. She trailed her fingers down his neck, following them with her mouth and tongue.

He cradled her head in one hand and groaned low in his throat as she slid farther down, getting into position to lave and suck on his nipple.

Good, she thought. She had him. She slid her leg up his and nearly moaned herself when she felt his erection pulse.

Flattening her hand against his rib cage, which rose and fell rapidly with his breaths, she tasted his skin, inch by inch, as she crept toward his left nipple.

Then her lips hit a rough spot.

She froze.

Rook's fingers curled inward, fisting in her hair. "Irina, I tried—"

She sucked in a long breath. It cleared her head. Her sleepy, erotic haze vanished.

She looked at his chest and saw the round, rough-edged scar where the bullet had hit him.

"No," she whispered as the swirling special world dissolved and the nightmare trapped her again. The nightmare that had haunted her for two years.

Rook, rising above her, moving within her, then sinking into the dark bloody waters of the Mediterranean.

She raised her gaze to meet his eyes. They burned into hers and she knew that this was no nightmare. It was her life.

"Please," she begged. "Stop haunting me."

A strong arm tightened around her bare shoulder. Panic built inside her. Why couldn't she wake up?

"Irina, shh. It's okay. I'm here."

His voice slid through her like the reverberation of a kettle drum—low, ringing, real. His breath whispered across her cheek.

She was in his arms, her head resting in the hollow of his shoulder. He was here.

No. She shook off the fantasy. He wasn't here. Not really. He was dead. Her loving, gentle husband was dead. She'd been dreaming again.

Beneath her cheek, his chest expanded and he sighed. Her fingers tingled with the life, the vibrancy that pulsed beneath them.

He was here.

She stiffened. He'd come back from the dead, and brought danger with him. Danger to her, to himself, to the people who depended on them and cared about them.

She pushed away and sat up.

"Did you have a bad dream?"

She laughed. "A bad dream?" She pushed her fingers through her hair. "No. Not a bad dream. I am having a bad reality."

She scooted across the bed, away from him, alarmed at how easily and instinctively she'd gone to him and slept in his arms, as if he'd never been gone.

Desperately, she struggled to grasp onto reality. To think about anything other than her pathetic reaction to his presence.

"Oh— Brock." Something had happened to Brock. She rubbed her eyes and pushed her hair back. "Brock was shot? How is he?"

"He's fine. The bullet went through his biceps." Rook threw back the covers and got up with his back to her. He was dressed in nothing but briefs. He reached for his pants.

Irina's eyes went straight to the scar on his upper back. It was nothing like the neat circular scar on his chest. This one was jagged and ugly.

"What happened?" she asked.

He half turned as he finished zipping and buttoning the pants. "What?"

"There. Your back."

He grimaced. "The old farmer who saved me took the bullet out. He said it would poison me if it stayed in. Said he'd dug bullets out of his cows before, and a dog or two." He arched his shoulder, as if it hurt him. "He had trouble finding it."

The words hung in the air.

He had trouble finding it. A simple sentence, spoken calmly, no bitterness, no resentment. Certainly no whining. Just a fact.

It made her want to cry. Made her realize that she could never imagine the pain he'd gone through, or the loneliness.

"Did you—" She stopped. She couldn't even ask that question. He'd been out there alone for two years. If he'd found someone to share the lonely nights, could she blame him?

Something burned deep inside her. The hurt was so deep, so ingrained, that she thought nothing could make it worse, but the idea of him making love with someone else, of sharing even one night with another woman while she lay alone, thinking he was dead, hurt her through to her soul.

"Did I what?" He turned and glared at her. "Go ahead and ask. You've earned the right not to trust me."

She shook her head, swallowing hard against the lump that was growing in her throat and blinking away the stinging behind her eyes.

"I'll answer your questions, Rina. I told you I would. But could you hurry? I'm meeting Deke and Dan at seven."

"Did you have anyone to talk to?"

"That's what you wanted to ask?" He stared at her in disbelief. "The farmer was nice. But, no. I stayed away from people as much as possible. As I worked my way closer to Ordo's hideout, I became more visible because of my differentness, and the danger increased."

He headed for the dressing room. "Now, if there's nothing else," he said on a sigh, "I've got to shave." His gaze held hers for another instant, then faltered.

She didn't speak.

He stepped into the dressing room and closed the door.

When she heard the latch catch, the sob that she'd

been trying to swallow escaped, followed by another and another and another.

Her first thought upon coming face-to-face with him less than forty-eight hours ago was right.

She didn't know him at all.

Chapter Ten

By the time Rook showered, shaved and dressed, it was six-thirty. He needed to get a move on if he was going to meet Deke and Dan at seven.

The light from the dressing room illuminated Irina's face. Her eyes were closed but he knew she wasn't asleep. The line of her body was stiff. Her eyelids quivered.

Because of him.

He clenched his teeth and gave his head a short shake. He had a lot to make up for, but it was going to have to wait. He looked at his watch. Quarter to seven.

Keys. He had no idea where keys to the cars might be. Hell, he didn't even know what cars they had. He started toward his dresser, but its surface was polished and empty.

If everything was the same as it had been when he left, there were extra keys to each vehicle hanging on hooks down in the garage. His mouth curled up at the irony. Everything the same? Hardly. Nothing was the same as it had been.

Just as he reached for the door handle, the phone rang. The sound slashed through him. Something else he was going to have to get used to again—all the sounds of America. Phones. Cars. Televisions. Buzzing and ringing and humming and blaring. The sounds of technology.

He grabbed the handset before it could ring a second time.

"Castle," he said.

Irina lifted her head, met his gaze briefly, then turned over.

"This is Taylor. We've got an explosion at the Treasury Building."

Rook instinctively snapped into emergency mode. "Casualties?"

"Unknown. I'm on my way there. I'm calling Cunningham on his cell now."

"I'll be there in ten." He hung up with a curse.

"Rook?" She sat up and pushed her hair out of her face. "What happened?"

"There's been an explosion in town, at the building where the prisoners are being held." He pointed a finger at her. "Lock the door behind me. Don't use the phone. Don't open the door. Not for anybody."

"Who do you think—"

"Do you understand?"

She frowned and lifted her chin. "Yes, sir. But how will I know—"

For a fraction of a second, Rook paused. But time to reassure her was time that could be used to catch the person responsible for the blast.

"I'll call you," he snapped, then turned on his heel and left, locking the door behind him.

EVERYTHING WAS ready. He was just waiting to hear that the diversion went as planned. He looked at his watch. It should have happened twenty minutes ago.

His room phone rang. Taking a deep breath, he picked up the phone.

"We have an incident." It was Brock with his typical terseness.

"An incident?" he said drowsily.

"Explosion at the Treasury Building. Rook's on his way."

"I'll get dressed."

"Stay there in case this is a diversion."

"Yes, sir." He fumbled as he hung up the phone. His hands were shaking that badly. He already had the prepaid cell phone in his pocket, along with his passport, all the money he'd managed to save and one photo. He looked around the room. Nothing else mattered. He was on his way to his new life.

He looked at his watch. He had forty minutes to kill, then he'd walk down the hall to his fellow specialist's room and inform him of the phone call he'd just received from Rook, outlining a change of plans.

In slightly over twenty-four hours, the finders fee would be his, his personal mission would be accomplished.

IRINA PACED BACK and forth. It had been over an hour since Rook left. She'd showered and dressed. She should have heard something by now. Rook had had plenty of time to get into town and check out the damage.

She understood why he'd told her to keep the door locked until he got back. What she didn't understand was why she couldn't make a phone call. Of course he could call her any minute, but one brief call to find out what had happened wasn't going to hurt anything. In fact, she could use her cell and not even tie up the house phone.

She could call Aimee out in the guesthouse and ask if she'd heard anything from Matt.

But her cell wasn't on the charger, and it wasn't in her purse. She must have left it in her office after she'd called her accountant yesterday—no, the day before. Wednesday.

She picked up the phone on her bedside table. She didn't know which room Aimee and Matt were in, but she could call the main guesthouse number.

Then she spotted the phone book on the lower shelf of the bedside table. The hospital. *Mindy*—she'd know what was going on, if anyone did.

Just as she pressed the first number, a knock came at the door.

Thank heavens. He was finally back. She hung up and rushed over to the door, but stopped with her hand on the deadbolt.

"Rook?" she called through the door. "Is that you?"

"Irina? It's Rafe. Aaron's here. Colonel Castle sent us to get you."

"Rafe? Aaron? Why? What has happened? What about Rook? Is he okay?"

"He's fine, ma'am. We're to bring you into town, to the Vick Hotel."

"What? He told me to stay here. Why didn't he call me?"

After a minuscule pause, Aaron spoke up. "He did. On your cell. You didn't answer."

Irina unlocked the door and looked at the two earnest young men. "What happened? Where is he?"

"Still at the explosion site," Aaron said. "There were several casualties. They're digging them out."

"Oh, no. Not anyone we know?"

Aaron glanced at Rafe.

"Oh, no. Who?" Irina picked up a jacket that matched her outfit.

Aaron led her out, with Rafe following. "Two of the Secret Service agents were injured, and one of the suspects."

They went down to the basement, where Aaron grabbed the keys to the Yukon. "Get in the back, Irina. You'll be safer back there."

Aaron climbed into the driver's seat and Rafe got in on the passenger side. When Aaron started the engine, an annoying beeping began.

"Seat belts," he said.

Irina pushed the belt's clasp into the lock. It seated easily.

Aaron glanced in the rearview mirror.

"What about Aimee?" Irina asked. "And her baby? She's in the guesthouse."

"One of the Secret Service agents is going to drive them to the Vick, too. But Rook gave us specific instructions to bring you through the delivery entrance in back of the hotel." Aaron started the engine and reached up to dial in the code that opened the garage door.

"Ah, hell," he said under his breath.

"What?" Rafe asked.

"We're supposed to reset the password on the garage door." He sighed and reached to unfasten his seat belt. "We should have been out of here five minutes ago."

"I'll set it," Rafe said.

"Let me watch. I can't remember the sequence."

Aaron jumped out, then bent and leaned back in. "We'll be right back, Irina. You sit tight."

"That's what I'm doing," she responded with a tiny smile.

Aaron and Rafe disappeared through the metal door into the safe room.

Several seconds later, Aaron came out alone. He sent Irina a small smile as he got in and started the engine. He opened the garage door.

A twinge of apprehension hit Irina just beneath her breastbone. "What about Rafe?"

"He decided to stay here and guard the house."

"But you said Rook sent you both."

"I did."

Aaron glanced in the rearview mirror at her, his expression stony, his eyes glittering.

Her apprehension grew. "I don't understand."

Aaron turned the car around and drove up the driveway to the road.

"You will." His voice took on a hard quality. His fingers whitened around the steering wheel.

Alarm arrowed through her. "Please let me use your phone. I want to call Rook."

"I'm afraid I can't do that right now."

"Aaron, what is going on?"

He didn't answer as he pulled out of the driveway onto the road.

"What has happened to Rafe? Where are you taking me?"

"You need to calm down, Irina. Everything's going to be all right."

It wasn't all right. She knew it wasn't. Aaron was driving too fast. He was acting too odd.

"What happened to Rafe?"

He glanced at her in the rearview mirror. "Rafe didn't have your best interests at heart."

Rafe? "What do you mean? Is Rafe the traitor?" She'd hired him. If he was in league with Novus Ordo, then she'd caused all the injuries, the deaths. The awful things that had happened were her fault.

"That's what *I'd* call him."

"What did you do to him?"

"Nothing permanent. He was trying to put you in harm's way, so I had to incapacitate him, and I had to make it bad enough to put him out of commission for a while. I kicked him in the thigh and locked him in the conference room."

Shock flashed through her like lightning. "I don't understand. What did he do?"

"Let's just say he has his own agenda."

"His own—?" Irina had never gotten to know Aaron very well. He was always polite, but he'd rarely spoken to her unless she deliberately engaged him in conversation. She'd decided that he was painfully shy around women.

But he was acting odd, even for him. And something didn't feel right about this whole thing.

Rook's warning echoed in her brain. *Lock the door and don't open it to anyone but me.*

"Please let me use your phone, Aaron. I want to talk to my husband."

"Not now," he snapped. "I'm sorry. I don't mean to yell at you. But things are a little tense and I'm on a very tight schedule. You'll get to talk to him just as soon as we're safe."

Aaron slowed down to pull into the left lane at the intersection of Midway Road and Highway 43.

"Aaron wait. You turn right to get to the Vick Hotel."

He didn't respond, but when the left arrow lit, he pulled forward and turned left.

"Aaron, stop this car immediately!"

He shook his head without turning around.

"Aaron!" Irina reached for her seat belt. She punched the release button, but nothing happened. She punched it again. And again.

Twisting, she tried to examine it. She didn't see anything physically wrong with it. But no matter how she tugged and struggled, she couldn't get it to unlock.

"Aaron, I can't get the seat belt off."

"Don't worry about it. We'll be there in a few minutes."

"Be where? Aaron, talk to me. What are you doing?"

But he didn't speak.

Panic burned her temples and scalp. Her fingers shook with dread knowledge. She was being kidnapped.

Aaron was the traitor.

They were approaching another intersection.

Please turn red, she begged the light. *Please. Come on.*

The light turned yellow. For a split second, Aaron held on to his speed, but a big truck approached from their right, so he had to slow down.

The light turned red.

Send a car, she prayed. *Please. Give me a chance to attract someone's attention.*

But they sat there alone. Irina kept her eyes on the back of Aaron's head as she tried to slide excess seat belt through, to give her enough room to slide out of the constraining straps. But there was something wrong with the automatic locking mechanism. She couldn't pull but an inch or so of strap through before the lock engaged. She kept working.

Just then a car drove up beside them—on the driver's side—opposite of where she sat behind the passenger seat.

Forgetting caution or threats, she leaned as far to her left as she could and waved her arms and shouted.

"Help! Help me!" She stretched as far as she could, but the wide seats of the huge SUV made it impossible for her to bang or even tap on the window.

"Help!" she screamed.

"Irina, you're wasting your time and your breath. Nobody's going to take you seriously. Besides, the glass is tinted so dark that they can barely see you anyway. You're wasting your strength, too, and I promise you you're going to need it."

The light turned green and the other car sped away, oblivious of Irina and her plight.

As Aaron pulled away, she leaned forward as far as she could and tried to beat on Aaron's head and neck with her fists. She was barely able to touch him, much less hurt him. The best she could do was distract him.

"If you don't stop," he threatened, "I'll stop the car. Believe me, you'll regret it if I do."

She thought about it. If he stopped the car, at least she'd have a chance she didn't have now. But the tone of his voice told her that she was at best a noisy annoyance. He was in too much of a hurry. He wasn't about to waste time stopping the car.

So she looked around the seat and the floorboard. Usually, there was an umbrella lying behind the driver's seat. But, no. He must have inspected the SUV and cleaned it out.

The center armrest was closed. Maybe someone had left a pen or a mini-umbrella in there. But it was empty, too.

"Settle down, Irina. We're almost there."

"You go to hell!" she shouted, and kept punching at him. "Almost where?"

She looked at her shoes. She was wearing loafers. Not even a high heel for a weapon.

The car careened to the right. She looked up and knew where they were heading. The only thing on this road for miles was a small airfield.

Oh, no. "No," she gasped. "Aaron, what are you doing?"

He ignored her, pulling a cell phone from his pocket. He dialed a number and paused, then spoke. "We're here."

The voice on the other end of the phone was barely audible. Irina couldn't make out anything that was said.

By the time the conversation was over, Aaron had pulled up beside a dilapidated hangar.

"Aaron—please. Do not do this. You will be in so much trouble. Kidnapping is a federal crime."

He stopped the car and turned around, amusement lighting his dark features. "A *federal* crime?" He shook his head. "Really, Irina, surely by now you know that a U.S. federal kidnapping charge is the least of my worries."

Then the reality hit. The truth she'd managed to deny until this moment.

Aaron wasn't just kidnapping her. He was taking her out of the country.

He was taking her to Novus Ordo. She was going to be bait to lure Rook to his death.

A deep, visceral fear shrouded her, taking the place of the panic. Aaron had fooled everyone, including Deke and Rook.

"You don't want to do this, Aaron. When they catch you, they will execute you."

"They'll have to find me first. I'll be safe with Ordo."

"Why, Aaron? You're an American citizen. Why are you betraying your own country?"

He turned in his seat to look at her.

"My country? My country isn't America. My country is Israel. My relatives were killed in the Holocaust." His eyes burned with obsessive zeal. "And your famous husband—do you know where his family came from? They came from Germany."

"You can't believe that Rook—"

"I can and I do. Do you know that he killed my father? He let him *die*. Norman Gold was a hero. And Castle let him die like an ordinary grunt. Then he had the gall to hire me, as if it made up for what he'd done. For what his ancestors did."

"Oh, Aaron. Rook was devastated about your dad. He felt responsible for you—"

Aaron cut her off with a string of curses, then got out of the car. When he did, Irina saw the two men dressed in black with black ski masks over their faces approaching.

Aaron spoke to them and nodded. The three had a brief conversation. Then Aaron gestured back toward the car.

Irina tugged at the door handle, but nothing happened. She pressed the UNLOCK button, then tried it again, pulling on the handle and pushing her shoulder against the door.

It wouldn't budge. She couldn't tell if it was locked or somehow jammed. "Come on. Open," she whispered desperately.

How had Aaron managed to sabotage the SUV without anyone noticing?

She answered her own question. Aaron was their computer expert. He'd have no problem disabling or avoiding the security cameras. With everything that had been going on, and the fact that the specialists had always had unrestricted access to the ranch house, it was no wonder that Aaron had found time to break the auto-release on the seat belt and activate the child-proof locks. She even understood why he'd chosen the Yukon. It was huge, with ultra-dark tinted windows. He could sneak her out past the guards with no trouble.

She should have anticipated this. Should have planned for any contingency. After all, Rook had warned her.

But seeing Aaron and Rafe at her door, looking so solemn and earnest, had fed right into her fear that something had happened to Rook. She'd been so worried that she hadn't even grabbed her purse. She didn't have any money or any ID. Maybe that was a good thing. Maybe it would make it difficult for Ordo to get her out of the country.

As the two masked men stalked toward the car, she braced herself. As soon as they opened the door, she'd start screaming. Surely there was someone around the airfield who would hear and come to the aid of a woman in distress.

One of the men reached for the door handle. The other took something out of his pocket.

She took a deep breath.

When the first man opened the door she screamed at the top of her lungs—for about half a second.

Then the second man clapped a wet cloth over her face, muffling her voice. She grabbed his wrist, doing her best to push him away, gasping and coughing at the sweet, acidic smell of whatever was on the cloth.

She held her breath and struggled as long as she could. It felt like a long time, but she figured it was only seconds. The man holding her was strong. Very strong.

Finally she had to breathe. The caustic vapor burned all the way through her throat to her lungs. She coughed again, weakly, and gagged. Despite her best efforts, her hands fell away from the man's thick wrists.

Her last coherent thought was that they would need a knife to get the seat belt undone.

Chapter Eleven

The Sundance fire chief pointed toward the smoking pile of rubble that had been the east end of the ground floor of the Treasury Building. "You see how the blast took out all of the first floor on this side, but only a small portion of the second floor? That's the danger. Now there's nothing supporting the second and third floors."

Rook nodded and turned to Taylor. "Is it confirmed that there were no casualties?"

"A couple of agents have bruises and minor burns, but this end of the building was empty. Makes you wonder if whoever set the explosive knew that, or if he just couldn't get inside the building."

"Yeah," Rook responded. "This is the least visible spot, back here next to the parking lot. Could be why they chose it."

The fire chief shifted from one foot to the other. "That's what we'll be able to determine, once it cools off enough to get inside. Meanwhile, I need to check and be sure everyone's been evacuated."

"The prisoners have been taken to Casper," Taylor said. "And my men will relocate to Castle Ranch."

"I'll tell you right now," the chief continued. "I'm sure we're going to have to blow the building. This area's too unsafe to leave it as is. The safest thing will be to bring the building down. So as soon as I can let you in to pull out all your papers and equipment, I'll let you know."

Taylor nodded. "Thanks."

Rook checked his watch. "I need to call Irina, let her know everything's all right."

Dan handed him his phone. "Go ahead."

Rook dialed the private line that only rang in their suite, but there was no answer.

A sick dread settled under his breastbone.

"Dammit, Rina," he mouthed. "I told you—" He stopped. She wouldn't have left. He knew it. Something had happened.

"I've got to get back to the ranch, now!"

There must have been something in his voice, because both the fire chief and Dan turned and stared at him.

"Let's go," Dan said. "I'm going with you."

On the way, Dan made several rapid phone calls. "No one entered or left through the main gate. Your housekeeper is checking your suite and Lieutenant Parker is trying to locate Gold and Jackson."

Rook turned into the driveway that led to the underground garage. He hit the high-security garage-door opener and pulled inside.

"There's a car missing…I think," he said as he screeched to a halt at the entrance of the garage and jumped out. "The Yukon."

He pointed to the empty space as he jogged past, heading for the conference room. The elevator there was the most efficient way to get upstairs.

As he got close enough to see, he noticed that the

safety door separating the garage from the conference room was ajar.

"Dammit." He stopped in his tracks and held up his fisted hand, signaling Dan to stop and nodding toward the door. The Secret Service agent drew his handgun.

Rook was forced to hang back while Dan went into the conference room first.

"Clear," Dan called. Then in the next breath, "Jackson!"

As Rook rounded the corner, he saw Dan bending over a crumpled figure lying in a pool of blood.

"It's Rafe Jackson," Dan said. He tossed his cell phone to Rook. "Call 911. Looks like somebody smashed his thigh. Damn."

Rook dialed and reported to the 911 operator what they needed, then called the gate to let them know an ambulance was on its way.

"Can you handle this?" he asked Dan. "I've got to check on Irina."

Dan nodded. "Go."

Rook rode the elevator to the executive office. Then he raced through the house to the east wing.

Just as he feared, the suite was empty. Irina's purse sat on her dresser. But there were no signs of a struggle, and no blood. Thank God for that.

His cell phone rang. "Yeah?"

"Colonel Castle? This is Special Agent Shawn Cutler. I just received word back from the FBI. They've got a match for Frank James."

Rook started to interrupt him, but he needed this information. It would help him find whoever had abducted Rina.

"His name is Franklin Hill, age forty-three. No criminal record."

"How'd they get his prints?"

"Seems he worked one summer for the Forest Service."

"Get the full report to Taylor. Right now I've got a situation."

"Yes, sir."

"And, Cutler, see what you can dig up about his relatives. Specifically if he has a brother." Rook hung up.

So Novus Ordo's real name was Hill.

"You did this," he said aloud. "Didn't you, *Novus Ordo?* But how?" Irina wouldn't have gone without a fight—unless she knew and trusted the person.

Rafe was downstairs, fighting for his life. Matt and Deke were accounted for. It had to be Aaron Gold or Brock O'Neill.

He slammed his palm against the door facing, putting his weight behind it. "Damn you, Novus. You win, for now. I'm coming to get my wife. But don't think for a minute that you've won the war." He flexed his throbbing hand.

"In a little while I'm going to know exactly who you are. And I'm coming after you."

IRINA'S HEAD WAS pounding and her stomach felt queasy. She opened her eyes, but it didn't help. Wherever she was, it was dark as hell. And cold.

The last thing she recalled was a wet cloth over her face and a sweetish odor that burned her throat, turned her stomach and knocked her out. Something not quite remembered made her think the liquid was ether.

She sat up, groaning. She tried to stretch her legs, but something was in the way.

She recoiled when she heard metal scrape against

metal, and a sliver of light appeared in front of her. Someone was opening a door.

Blinding light hurt her eyes, before a shadow blocked it. A man loomed over her.

"Who are you?" she rasped. Her throat burned. "Where am I?"

He didn't say anything. He grabbed her upper arm.

She wanted to fight, but she was too drowsy, and her limbs felt like they were made of lead. She felt a sharp prick and then a burning pain.

"Ouch!" She tried to jerk her arm away, tried to kick him, but she didn't have enough room to put any strength behind it.

He grunted. She'd like to think with pain, but she had a sinking feeling he was laughing at her. He withdrew, and for the few seconds the light shone in, she tried to make sense of what she saw. Dark metal with bumps on it. Wooden crates and canvas bags stacked all around her. Then the light disappeared.

A bitter taste suffused her mouth. Her eyelids wouldn't stay open. She tried to push herself up into a sitting position. Tried to sing, stretch, anything to stay awake, but she couldn't fight the drug.

THE NEXT TIME she woke up, the bitter taste was still with her, and the inside of her mouth felt like cotton. Her limbs were stiff and sore. A dull ache drummed in her temples—like a hangover headache.

She opened her eyes—a chore, because she was so drowsy—and found herself in a tiny, dismal room, lying on a narrow bed with threadbare sheets and a thin blanket. On the other side of the room, the midday sun shone blindingly hot through a small window with broken glass.

The room smelled of sweat and sand and heat. The air was still, oppressively still. She felt claustrophobic, smothered, like she couldn't breathe. She sucked in a lungful of warm air. It didn't help.

She closed her eyes, but that made her stomach flip over, so she sat up, groaning at her stiff, achy muscles, and rubbed her face and eyes. A fine grit under her fingertips scraped her skin, like sand or salt. She tasted it. Salt. The hot, dry air was drawing all the moisture out of her skin.

She licked her dry lips and grimaced when she tasted more salt. Squinting against the sun's glare, she checked out her surroundings. The room was barely big enough for the bed and a small scarred table. She saw a glass jar of water sitting on it.

She whimpered aloud as she reached for the jar, ready to turn it up and pour the liquid down her throat.

But the memory of the foul, nauseatingly sweet-smelling cloth and the prick of the needle stopped her.

What if the water was drugged?

Her throat spasmed and her jaw ached. She craved the liquid so badly that she didn't care.

In this awful place that looked and smelled like hell, maybe she'd be better off asleep.

Without pausing to taste it first, she turned the jar up and drank. The water was flat and lukewarm and slightly brackish, but it was wet.

When she'd drunk all she could, she poured some in her cupped hand and splashed it on her face and eyes. It washed away a little of the salt and drowsiness that clung to her.

Pushing herself to her feet, she walked weakly over to the window. She'd expected to find herself on the second or third floor to prevent an escape. But the room looked right out onto the street. The cracked window was coated with dust and sand. Still, she could see through it.

The latch was rusted. She tried it. It squeaked and she let go as if it were hot. Apparently it still worked.

All she would have to do was turn the latch, push the window open and slip through it. Then she could run. Find someone to help her. Maybe to take her to the American embassy.

But as she studied the scene before her, she realized that there would be no one to help her in this town. The United States didn't put embassies in small towns like this.

How impossibly naive she was. It was obvious why her captors hadn't bothered to secure the window.

The dull gray scene before her gave her the answer. So what if she did escape? What would she be escaping to? A dusty barren alien land, where women were draped from head to toe in dark, hot burkas. Where men stalked the streets dressed in military garb with menacing weapons cradled in their arms and ammunition belts draped across their torsos. Or slunk from doorway to doorway, wall to wall, dressed in rags, with fear and defeat in their eyes.

Her choices for shelter were buildings riddled with bullet holes and draped with barbed wire strung like Christmas lights, or mud huts less sturdy than where she was now.

She was in a Muslim town—a Muslim country. A place halfway around the world from Wyoming.

Out of habit, she glanced at her left wrist. Her watch! She'd been unconscious for over twenty-four hours.

She touched the watch's crystal, remembering when

Rook had given it to her on their first anniversary. She still had her rings, too. The beautiful diamond solitaire and wedding band.

It terrified her that the people who had kidnapped her had no interest in jewelry that could buy them enough food for a year.

She began to feel eyes on her. Some of the people slinking along the street spotted her. A child in rags with bare feet and a grimy face pointed in her direction. A burka-wrapped woman walked past her window. Her eyes widened when she met Irina's gaze through the smeared glass.

Irina backed away and sat down on the bed. It took some thought, but she finally forced her blurry brain to piece together what had happened to her.

Aaron Gold had kidnapped her. Aaron, whom Rook had hired after his father had died under Rook's command.

She knew Rook felt responsible for him, because of his father's death. And Aaron admired Rook. He'd never given any indication that he resented him. He'd always seemed fascinated by Rook's stories about his dad. He'd always acted grateful.

Had his quiet shyness been a mask to cover his true self? The expression he'd worn as he drove off with her in the Yukon had been hard and sinister.

He hadn't blinked an eye as the two men drugged her. She didn't know what had happened next, but she could imagine.

After they'd knocked her out, they'd put her on a plane, probably a small one, judging by the cramped space.

After that she remembered almost nothing. How had they taken her from that small plane to one big enough to cross the Atlantic? How had they smuggled her out of the country? Where was the security that America was so proud of, if a few men could steal a person and get them out of the country unnoticed?

Of course, she had no way of knowing whether alarms had been triggered. Homeland Security, the Secret Service and the USCIS could all be looking for her at this very moment.

Rook could be looking for her.

She waited for the sense of relief to flood her at that thought, but it didn't come.

She looked down at herself. She was still dressed in the slacks and shirt she'd had on when Aaron and Rafe had knocked on her door. Her shirt was sweat stained and wrinkled, and the black slacks were gray with dust. Her jacket was gone, as were her loafers. At least they hadn't undressed her.

A noise outside the door made her jump. Then the rusty sound of a key turning in a lock.

Irina moved to the far side of the room in front of the window. She wasn't sure what she thought that would accomplish. Maybe if someone saw her being attacked, they'd come to her aid?

Judging by the eyes of the people she'd seen, they were too afraid to risk helping her.

Two men in military garb entered the room with weapons in arms. One carried a length of dark cloth. The first man, the one in charge, yelled gibberish at her. Then he looked at the other man and jerked his head.

The soldier tossed the dark cloth at her feet. Then the one in charge pointed at it and yelled some more.

Irina looked down at the cloth. Was this a burka? She had no idea, but she wasn't about to put on that heavy, hot cloak over her clothes, and she wasn't about to take off her clothes.

So she looked up at the man in charge and spat a few choice phrases at him in Russian.

His heavy, dark brows went up in surprise. He muttered something and then gestured at the other soldier with his head.

The soldier said something back to him. He half turned and cocked his weapon, and the soldier held up a hand. He slung his rifle over his shoulder by its strap and started toward Irina.

She crossed her arms. "I am not taking my clothes off," she said in English.

The soldier didn't react. He merely picked up the length of cloth and held it out.

She shrugged.

The one in charge said something that Irina was sure would translate to "Hurry up. We don't have all day."

The soldier shook out the cloth and snapped at her.

All she could think of to do was shrug again.

He held his hand up, forefinger down, and made a twirling motion.

With a glance at the other soldier, she obeyed. She'd shown them she was no pushover—she hoped—but she didn't want to make them angry enough to hurt her.

When her back was to him, he draped the cloth over her head and shoulders. Then he spoke again.

After an instant's hesitation, she turned back around. He wrapped the burka around her until she felt like a mummy.

At least they didn't take her clothes off.

The man in charge gave her an order, and the second man nudged her with his rifle.

Irina stood her ground and pointed to her bare feet. "Where are my shoes?" That earned her another nudge.

They forced her out the door, where the soldier pointed at the floor.

Her shoes. Thank heavens. She slipped her feet into them gratefully. From what she'd seen of the streets outside, she did *not* want to walk out there barefooted.

She was hustled out of the building and into a dusty, battered Jeep. She kept her eyes closed for the entire trip. She even dozed off a few times—thanks to all the sedatives she was sure were still in her body.

When the Jeep came to a halt, she opened her eyes, and wanted to cry. They were parked in front of a tent, set against the side of a mountain and surrounded with armed guards.

She was ordered out of the Jeep and manhandled through the flap. Inside was dark and heavily scented with incense.

All Irina could see were flickering candle flames, and even those were pale and dim. A rifle barrel nudged her in the back again, causing her to stumble forward. She put her hands out, afraid of the dark, afraid she was going to walk into something. Around her she heard the rustle of clothes, the creak of leather, metal scraping against metal, people breathing. The same sounds she'd listened to while traveling in the Jeep with the two soldiers.

The gunman behind her kept nudging her forward. She moved slowly, shuffling, still afraid she would trip and fall. Then the toe of one loafer slammed into something. It felt like rock.

As her eyes adapted to the darkness, she saw the difference in the color of the ground beneath her feet. The road outside, and the floor of the tent, was dirt, but now she was stepping onto rock. Big rocks, smooth rocks.

Then, from in front of her, a voice barked orders in

the same language the soldiers had used, and the two soldiers backed away, leaving her standing alone.

She was becoming more accustomed to the dim candlelight. It helped her to see, but the smell of tallow was making her queasy.

The farther she went into what she could only guess was a cave, judging by the stone floor, the more candles lit her way and the hotter the air grew.

Slowly, the outline of a man in light-colored robes came into focus. He was sitting above and in front of her, on some kind of raised platform. His face looked unnaturally pale in the candlelight.

She blinked and looked around her. She could make out several soldiers standing or sitting in the darkness. She could see the candlelight glinting off their weapons and the belts of bullets.

Turning back to the pale man, she spotted a woman in a glittering dress sitting on the floor at his feet. She looked from the woman's sepia-toned face to the man's.

There was something strange about his face—she couldn't see his features. Just his eyes and that pale... mask.

Mask.

The heat, the smell of many bodies in a hot close place and the weight of the burka on her head and shoulders made her head spin.

The man barked another order. Someone grabbed the burka and yanked it off of her, almost knocking her off her feet. Then a blow to the backs of her calves sent her sprawling backward onto a cushioned surface. She'd landed on some kind of upholstered stool.

"Take a load off, Mrs. Castle."

Alarm ripped through her like lightning. English?

She cast about. Who was speaking in English—and American English at that?

As quickly as her gaze snapped to his featureless face, her brain told her the answer.

Novus Ordo. It had to be. The CGI image Rook had described popped into her head, followed by the photo of the dead Frank James.

A pale mask. An American accent. A hidden cave in the farthest regions of the world. Of course it was Novus Ordo.

And with the help of a once-trusted employee, he'd captured her to lure Rook here.

And he would come. Not necessarily for her sake—although she had to believe that he cared enough to want to save her—but because finding her would mean finding Ordo. And she knew that would happen. Because Ordo had brought her here as bait to force Rook to come to him.

"No, it's not some man behind the curtain. It's me."

"Am I supposed to know who you are?" she asked, doing her best to affect an attitude of disinterest.

He laughed. "Supposed to? No. You *do* know who I am. Just as well as I know who you are. Can I get you some water?"

"No."

"Okay, but you're going to get awful thirsty. I might forget to ask you again."

"What do you want with me?"

"Now, come on, Mrs. Castle, you know that, too. You are here so you'd bring your nosy, arrogant husband to me."

Irina folded her hands in her lap and tried not to look as terrified as she felt. She knew the terrorist was ruthless. She'd seen what he'd already done and tried to do.

She'd listened along with Rook to the news stories recounting Ordo's terrorist attacks. The power plants, oil tankers and who knew what else?"

The man she knew only as Novus Ordo looked at his watch. "It's getting late," he said. "Let's go ahead and make that call. I've waited a long time to get my hands on him."

He snapped an order in that language she couldn't understand, and a soldier stepped out of the darkness to hand him a satellite phone.

Irina squeezed her hands together tightly. Maybe in the shadow of her lap, Ordo wouldn't see her white knuckles and know how scared she was.

He stood up. Immediately, all the people in the room stood. It was a sign of respect. Irina didn't stand.

One of the guards grabbed her arm and yanked her to her feet.

"*Nyet,*" she exclaimed, pulling her sleeve away from his grasp. Then she glared at Ordo. "What will you do if I refuse? Exile me to a worse place than this? To a life lonelier than mine has been for the past two years? *Kill* me?" She stood and crossed her arms.

"I'll do all of that, and more, if it helps me reach my goal. How do you think your husband would feel if I sent him one of your fingers? Or an ovary?"

Irina felt the blood drain from her face. She shivered at the icy chill that ran down her spine. She looked into Novus Ordo's eyes and remembered Jung's words. *If you stare into the abyss long enough, the abyss stares back at you.*

"Why are you doing this?" she cried. "What has Rook, what has the United States, done to you?"

Ordo smiled benignly. "Your husband saw my face. That's enough to condemn him. But the U.S. What has the U.S. done? The U.S. continues to ignore the dangers to the environment that they are perpetrating, not just on home soil but all over the world."

Irina stared, astonished. She wasn't sure what Ordo was talking about.

"Do you know who I am? I graduated magna cum laude from MIT in environmental engineering. My IQ is over 180. If they would just listen to me, I could save the planet. Did you know that within the next decade we could see the demise of every species of insect?"

"Insect?"

Novus snorted. "You have no idea what I'm talking about. Let's get back to what I'm going to do to your husband. You heard what I planned for you. Take that to the next level, and you'll understand what I'll do to Colonel Castle if you don't cooperate. Because you know he'll come. You know that. If you help me, I promise to execute Colonel Castle with dignity—by firing squad."

For a moment, Irina couldn't tear her gaze away from his. He didn't have to say the specific words for her to know what torture he implied. Her knees collapsed and she fell back onto the stool, gagging. She'd vomit if she had any food in her stomach.

Distantly she heard Novus say something. A white cloth was thrust under her nose. She used it to wipe her mouth and eyes, then she looked up at Novus.

"*Ya sdyelayoo eto,*" she rasped. "*Vi gryaznaya svin'ya.*"

"You're talking in Russian again."

Irina lifted her head and swallowed against the nausea. "I will do it," she said as strongly as she could. "Whatever you say." She left off the last bit of her Russian comment. *You filthy pig.*

Chapter Twelve

Rook drove the dusty, beat-up Jeep through the narrow streets of Mahjidastan, his stomach churning at the remembered smells of heat, sweat, dung and dust.

He'd been through a lot in his career as a combat rescue officer. He'd seen and heard some awful things, but nothing he'd ever been through in his life had prepared him for the abject horror in Rina's voice on the staticky satellite phone twenty-four hours before.

Please, Rook, do what he says. You can't imagine what he'll do if you don't follow his instructions to the letter.

Sadly, he *could* imagine.

But the next thing she'd said had baffled him. She'd spoken in Russian, and he hadn't understood a syllable. Thank God he'd insisted that every call that came in from the moment Irina went missing be recorded.

When he'd played the recording for Tanya, a friend of hers in Casper, Tanya had been baffled, as well.

"The last bit says 'I love you,' of course. And the middle part essentially translates as "ecological technical degree." But *provyer'tye em ay'tye?*" She sighed. "Check something. Check mit? Does that make sense?"

He'd written it all down. He spoke it out loud, over and over and over.

Check em ay'tye. Ecological technical degree. I love you.

Check em ay'tye. Ecological technical degree. I love you.

Finally, the answer had coalesced in his brain.

They weren't words, they were letters. MIT. Massachusetts Institute of Technology!

A call to Dan to check MIT for graduates with the last name of Hill who'd majored in ecology hit pay dirt.

Frank James's fingerprints had traced him back to Laramie, Wyoming. His name was Franklin Hill, and he had a brother who'd attended Wyoming University and then graduated summa cum laude in environmental engineering from MIT.

Frederick Hill had graduated with a brilliant future ahead of him. But as of eight years ago, he'd disappeared off the face of the earth—no tax returns, no driver's license. Nothing.

Novus Ordo. Frederick Hill.

As soon as Rook hung up from talking to Dan, he went to see Deke and had a long, somber discussion with him. Then he caught a plane for Kabul—alone. He couldn't take the chance that anyone would stop him.

So now he was here, where Ordo wanted him. All he had to do was wait. Ordo would find him.

At the door to the rooming house, he paused and looked around. Not to familiarize himself with the town—it was burned into his memory forever—but to ensure that everyone in town knew he was here.

Ordo had ordered him here. He was here.

The number of curious stares he attracted didn't scare him. Rather, he scrutinized each one. Trouble was, all of the dark eyes had shadows in their depths. Any one of them could be Ordo's spy.

He sure as hell hoped so. It had been well over forty-eight hours since Aaron had abducted Irina. He had no time to waste.

Turning on his heel, he headed inside. Ironically, the old woman who ran the inn had put him in the same room he'd been in before. A frisson of disgust spread through him. He'd hoped never to see these dingy walls again.

Just like the last time he'd left his home with little hope of returning, he'd brought nothing of value with him, except his watch, his wedding ring and his Sig Sauer.

He fingered the ring. This time was different. This time, the thing he valued most was here, in this desolate corner of the world.

And nothing—not his inherited millions, not his accomplishments, not even his connections with people like the president of the United States—could save her. He had nothing but his wits. That and faith.

He lay down on the narrow bed and closed his eyes. He had nothing to do now but wait. He thumbed the smooth surface of his wedding ring, and his thoughts turned backward, to his childhood.

It seemed to him that everything he'd ever done had led him to this time and place.

How would his life have been different if he and Matt and Deke, his oath brothers, had never gotten caught in that storm? If a good and honorable man hadn't lost his own life that day to save four boys?

He'd have probably taken over his father's diverse and lucrative media conglomerates, instead of joining the Air Force. He'd likely have married a hometown girl and had a nice, safe, normal life.

He'd have never rescued Leonid Tankien. Never met and fallen in love with Tankien's daughter, Irina. He'd have never sat in the Oval Office and chatted with the president about covert missions to rescue innocent Americans. He'd certainly have never had to ask his friends to lay their lives on the line for him.

He didn't regret any of his choices except one. If he could live his life over again, he'd never lie to Rina. She deserved better. She always had.

The banging on the door startled him out of his daydream. He rolled off the bed, gun in hand. "Who is it?" he yelled.

The snarling answer was in Arabic.

His breath whooshed out in cautious relief. Soon he'd be in front of Ordo. He'd be able to see for himself that Irina was all right.

He called out one of the few phrases he'd learned in the local language. From what he'd been told, it translated loosely as "Hang on a minute."

Gripping his weapon, Rook unlocked the door. When he saw the soldiers in their desert camo with ammunition belts criss-crossing their chests and heavy guns cradled in their arms, he raised his hands, letting his gun dangle from his fingertips.

The guy in charge stepped close and knocked the gun away.

Interpreting what was expected of him, Rook spread his hands in surrender. One of the armed soldiers turned around and put his back to the door facing, obviously guarding the door. The other stepped inside and trained his rifle on Rook's midsection.

The leader gestured to Rook. His meaning was unmistakable. He wanted him to undress. Probably for a strip search.

Rook stood without moving.

The leader gestured a second time and snapped an order.

Rook shrugged, affecting a puzzled expression. The skin on the back of his neck prickled. He hoped like hell that the man would give up if he played dumb.

No such luck. The rifle barrel pushed painfully into Rook's side.

Fine. He gave in, praying that the men weren't sadistic. They weren't. The search was almost cursory and was over inside of two minutes.

As soon as he got his shirt buttoned, the leader pulled a square of cloth from a pocket and gestured for Rook to turn around.

He decided further delays would only hurt his own agenda, which was getting himself in front of Ordo as quickly as possible, so he obeyed.

Within seconds, he was blindfolded and his hands were tethered behind his back. He had to quell his instinct to fight. This was not about him. Certainly not about being a hero, or getting revenge.

He was a player in a much bigger undertaking. Sure, he was here to get Rina to safety. But as much as he wished he could just somehow grab her and go, she wasn't his primary mission.

He didn't resist as the soldiers led him outside and pushed him into the backseat of an open vehicle— probably a Jeep.

They were taking him to Novus Ordo. And everything—*everything*—depended on how he handled himself.

If he were a desperate international terrorist whose true identity was in danger of being uncovered, and the one man in the world who could destroy him were brought before him, he'd execute him on sight. But he wasn't Novus Ordo.

And the plan depended on his expatriated American's need to gloat.

Because Rook was offering him exactly what he wanted—with one caveat.

Let Irina live.

The ride was a long one, and bumpy. Blindfolded, and with his hands behind his back, he was at the mercy of the dysfunctional shocks in the Jeep. His exhausted body took a battering by the time the vehicle finally stopped. Judging by how long it took, and the condition of the roads they'd ridden, he figured they'd driven up several hundred feet in elevation into the mountains.

He was manhandled out of the Jeep and shoved forward. He shuffled and stumbled as he tried to stay upright. Every time he paused, feeling his way for his next step, a rifle barrel prodded him in the kidneys.

Through the blindfold and his closed lids, he could tell when they entered a dark shelter, probably a tent. The odors of too many bodies in too close a space, combined with sweetish incense and cigarette smoke, made his nose burn. The heat was oppressive, and it wasn't helped by all the candles that flickered redly in front of his closed lids.

The toes of his boots hit something solid. He fell forward. His knees landed on some sort of wooden riser, or step.

The soldier growled in the language Rook had heard a lot here in Mahjidastan.

From in front of him, he heard another voice. Same language, but sounding very different. Then the same voice greeted him, and he understood what the difference was.

"Colonel Castle. Nice of you to drop by."

The voice belonged to an American.

He was standing in front of Novus Ordo.

Ordo barked a command. Someone yanked off Rook's blindfold, although they left his hands tied. He raised his head, blinking, waiting for his eyes to finish adapting to the dark.

Then he saw Ordo, his pale face illuminated by the wan light of the flickering candles. His face with no mask.

It was the face from the sketch. Almost identical to the face from the autopsy photo of Frank James.

"Ordo," he breathed. He pushed himself backward, trying to get his feet under him so he could stand. He'd just about straightened when a staggering blow struck the back of his knees. He fell forward, banging his cheek on the hard wooden platform.

Ordo snapped an order, and a hand in his hair jerked him upright.

"Sorry, Colonel. My soldiers don't like to see me disrespected."

The man who named himself Novus Ordo, or "New Order," sat in a crudely built wooden chair draped with lengths of cloth in various tones. The candlelight rendered everything nearly monochromatic. Novus wore a plain white shirt and tan pants that had seen better days.

His head was bare. His matted light brown hair completed his resemblance to Frank James—Franklin Hill, his younger brother.

"Where's Irina?"

"I figured that would be your first question. Let's just say she's safe, for the moment. So what's your second question?"

"Where's Aaron Gold?"

"Okay, good one—and easy. Aaron was a big help. A *big* help, but he's outlived his usefulness."

The relief he'd felt at hearing that Irina was safe faded and was replaced with dread. He closed his eyes briefly. "You killed Aaron?"

"Not yet. I thought you'd enjoy watching. Just like I'm certain that Mrs. Castle will get a kick out of watching you die."

Rook clenched his jaw. Let the man get his jollies. He knew Ordo was trying to get a rise out of him, but Rook was not going to give him the satisfaction.

He tried to relax. If Novus could see something as subtle as a muscle tensing, then let him enjoy it.

"Let's hear your third question," Novus said.

"How many questions do I get?"

Novus's brows drew down and his jaw tightened in irritation. "As many as I want to give you. Until I get bored. And by the way, that question—*very* boring."

"What happens when you get bored?"

That amused him. "I have a question for you."

Rook nodded. "Okay," he said. Inside, he felt the swell of triumph in his chest. He'd figured it wouldn't take long for Novus to get around to talking about himself. To do what he'd done took the mind of a megalomaniac, the soul of a sociopath, the distorted assurance of a messianic delusion.

"Have you figured out why you haven't been able to identify me?"

"What makes you think we haven't?"

Novus rolled his eyes. "Oh, please. Give me some credit. If the United States had confirmed my identity, my face would be plastered all over the Internet and the TV, searching for people who knew me, who might still be in touch with me. And I have spies everywhere."

"Maybe we're smarter than that. How did you feel about your brother's death?"

Even in the dim light, Rook saw Novus's face darken. "That was unnecessary," he said. "And your mistake. You probably could have bullied him into talking. So I guess I should be happy he's dead."

Rook looked at him questioningly. "Can I ask another question?"

Novus sat back on his makeshift throne and crossed his legs. "Sure. I've got nowhere to be."

"What are you doing here? You don't seem like the type to embrace Islam, or enjoy these primitive conditions. What made you leave your cushy life to come and live like this?"

"Cushy life?" Novus's head snapped up and his eyes narrowed suspiciously.

Rook winced inwardly. He hadn't meant to go there—at least not yet.

"What are you talking about? What do you know about—" Ordo stopped, studying Rook.

Finally he smiled and shook his head. "Oh, no. You're just trying to get me riled. You don't know anything about me."

Rook thought fast. "I know that when you were a kid, you didn't dream of becoming a terrorist. I know you're fairly intelligent, and extremely clever. What's the attraction? The fame? The money?"

"Haven't you been paying any attention to my radio messages? My blogs on the demise of this planet? Why do you think I bombed that nuclear plant in India? And that supposedly *secret* chemical munitions warehouse in Mexico. Why do you think I took three American oil tankers hostage?"

"That was you?" Rook goaded.

That angered Novus. His face turned bright red. "Of course that was me. What the hell's wrong with you?"

Rook shrugged. "I guess I forgot. From what I understand, a lot of people think you're dead. It's been two years since you've carried out a major attack. So what was your problem with those places? The oil tankers carry fuel to move food and necessary supplies around the world. The nuclear plant brings electricity to hundreds of thousands of people who couldn't otherwise afford it. And that munitions plant? It produced one-third of the chemical munitions used by the U.S. and NATO nations to protect their people."

"Do you know what happens to the waste from those places—not to mention the waste from people's everyday lives? We're destroying our planet. At the rate we're going, we'll be lucky if any species of insect survive the next decade."

"And that's not a good thing?" Rook asked innocently.

Novus pressed his palms against his temples. "You're baiting me. You can't be that dumb. Without insects, the entire ecology of the planet will fall apart. Mankind—hell, *everything*—will be extinct."

"If I'm understanding you correctly, you're committing acts of terrorism to save the planet? I'm not quite sure I can make that leap. You're murdering hundreds—thousands—of people in order to what, save some insects?" It was all Rook could do to keep from smiling. Ordo was right. He *was* baiting him.

"You don't understand. How could you, with your narrow point of view and your privileged life? Don't think I don't know who your father is. Be thankful I haven't bombed his National News Network yet. Although I do have plans to see what I can do to get my hands on some of those millions, after I've sent your body and your wife's back to the U.S." He smiled benignly. "I wonder who inherits all that money when you and your wife are dead?"

Jennie. His baby sister. Rook used every ounce of strength in his body not to react. "You'll never have the chance, Novus."

Ordo laughed. "Tall words. You act brave. It's going to be interesting to see how brave you really are."

"Bring it on, Novus. Without your rag-tag bunch of soldiers, I doubt you can hold your own."

"These hyenas? They don't understand my real purpose. I don't expect them to. They're useful just like they are. They think they're fighting a holy war. Makes it easy to send them on suicide missions." He stood and walked around the wooden chair and leaned on the back of it.

"Everyone is so hot on their religious icons," he continued. "They think Allah is their savior. Christians think Jesus is." He shook his head.

Rook frowned. "What do you think?" he asked, pretty sure he knew the answer.

Ordo thumped his chest. "I am the savior. I'm the only one who can really solve the world's problems. I tried to explain to your wife. No one would listen to a new PhD graduating in environmental engineering. Not even at MIT. I advocated for change. I wrote papers. I testified before Congress. I did everything I could to convince people that the destruction of the planet is almost out of hand."

Novus doubled his fists and pounded on the back of the chair. "I had no choice. They'll see. By the time I've taken out all the nuclear plants in the U.S., the world will know me and will see that I'm right. That I have saved the planet."

He was going to destroy over a hundred nuclear plants?

"You don't have the manpower to blow up a hundred plants at once."

"You have no idea."

With a start, Rook realized that the terrorist was right. There was no intel on how many followers Novus had.

"If you blow up all the nuclear plants in the U.S., you could potentially kill every person in North America."

"America is the biggest offender."

"When are you planning this attack?"

Ordo held up a finger. "Oh, no. Nobody knows the answer to that question. I trust my people, but not that much."

"I'm impressed, but I don't see you gathering enough people to carry out a plan like that."

Ordo yawned. "I'm bored. I thought you came here to rescue your wife."

Rook assessed the terrorist. What was he up to? "Of course, that's my top priority. But stopping you is a close second."

"Would you like to see her?"

Rook's throat seized. "Yes." He didn't trust himself to say anything more. He'd been so afraid that Ordo had hurt her, so afraid that he'd killed her already. He knew that all Ordo had wanted was to provide Rook with proof that he had her. It's why he'd forced her to call him. After that, Ordo had no reason to keep her alive.

"Good." Ordo came around the chair. "One thing I've never been accused of is being a bad host. Although you, Colonel Castle, are too big a liability to my cause and my anonymity, you obviously deserve some respect for your rank and your perseverance."

Rook waited, maintaining a neutral expression. At least so far, Novus had no idea his anonymity had been compromised.

"I've prepared my bedroom for you for tonight. Tomorrow morning I'm afraid I've got to execute you. But for now, I'm offering you a gesture of respect. Enjoy my hospitality, and enjoy your wife, on the last night of your life."

Rook laughed. "You've got to be kidding."

"No, sir. I am serious. It's a tradition amongst warriors. The night before the final battle should be spent in love. I'm offering you a warrior's final night."

There had to be a trick. Hidden cameras? Hidden microphones, in hope that he might whisper some secret plan to Irina?

"However," Ordo added.

And here it was. The trick.

"You'd do well to remember, Colonel Castle, that my bed is better guarded than any place in this entire province. If you try to escape, you'll be shot down like the mangy coyote you are. I'll put your head on a pike. And then I'll do what you failed to do. I'll enjoy your wife, right on top of your bloody corpse, before I leave her to my soldiers, who have few enough chances to see a beautiful woman such as her."

He took a deep breath and smiled. "Do I make myself clear?"

Rook looked Ordo full in the face and nodded. "I accept your offer."

Chapter Thirteen

Rook walked through a narrow passage into another candlelit room—an anteroom to the main cave, cut or worn into the mountain. It actually was set up as a bedroom.

Most of the candles were on wooden boxes that served as bedside tables for the surprisingly contemporary king-size bed. The mattress was draped with colorful quilts, spreads and pillows in jewel tones.

A carafe of water and one of wine sat on a low table beside the bed, along with bowls of figs and almonds.

On a low stool beside the bed was a porcelain chamber pot. The rest of the cave was bathed in darkness. Two candles flickered on a side table. In the glow, he made out a bowl and pitcher and a small stack of folded cloths.

Was this how Ordo lived, or had this ersatz honeymoon suite been put together for Rook's benefit?

More importantly—was Irina really here? Just as he asked himself that question, a shadow moved across the surface of the bowl and pitcher.

"Irina?" Her name was wrung from his throat unwillingly, in case Ordo was watching or listening. A testament to his fear and hope.

The shadow froze, then through the dimness a small figure moved toward him. The candlelight's glow picked up the person's silhouette, then began to chase the shadows away from the curves and planes of her body. *Her* body.

"Rina?" His voice broke.

"Rook?"

She stepped out of the shadows. She was dressed in a simple white *abaya* with embroidery across the front and down the sleeves. Her hair had been washed but not styled, so it floated like golden fog around her drawn face. Her blue eyes were huge and frightened.

He tore his eyes away from her and looked around the room, wishing he could somehow sense where microphones or cameras might be.

She touched his arm and gasped quietly. "You're really here."

His gaze snapped back to hers. He took a step forward and held out his hand.

For an instant she stared at his fingers as if she didn't quite know what to do, but then she laid her hand in his.

When she raised her frightened blue eyes to meet his, he tugged lightly, pulling her to him and wrapped his arm around her. For a few seconds, she just stood there, unmoving in his arms. Then he felt it, the giving in, the yielding. He knew she couldn't stay detached if he touched her. Just as he couldn't with her body pressed against his.

He embraced her fully, pressing her sweet familiar body to his, branding himself with her. How had he lived without her? Burying his nose in the sweet curve between her shoulder and neck, he knew the answer. He hadn't lived—he merely existed.

"Oh, Rook," she whispered. "Why did you come? Did you not figure my message?"

"Shh," he breathed in her ear, so low he couldn't hear himself. Then he nodded, twice.

Irina's breath blew out in a ragged sigh and her arms came up around his neck. "Then why—"

He tightened his arms. "Shh," he breathed again. "He could be listening."

She shook her head. "Nothing on me. I checked."

He was relieved. But what about him? Had the soldiers placed a bug on him during the strip search, or on the ride here? "Wait," he whispered.

He pulled away from her and shed his shirt, then brought his hand up around her neck and bent until his mouth was against her ear. "Check me."

She did, running her hands through his hair and down his neck. Over his shoulders, his upper arms, forearms and hands.

He stood stiffly, knowing the touching was necessary, knowing that losing himself in the soft caress of her fingers could be deadly, and yet unable to keep from reacting.

When she moved to his throat, his collarbone, his pecs, his heart rate went up and his breathing grew ragged. She wouldn't touch his nipples, would she? Not in this dangerous place as she performed such a dangerous job.

Her hands slid across his pecs and down his breastbone.

Then she did it. She ran her fingertips across his already distended nubs. He gasped. He lifted his hands to stop her before the intense shock of lust spread through his whole body, but he was already too late.

He groaned as his erection pulsed and grew.

She ran her fingers across his rib cage, his waist and his abdomen. When they touched the waistband of his pants, he caught her wrists.

"Back," he grated, and turned around. "If it's down there they won't be able to hear much."

She quickly checked his shoulders and back. When she was done, she pressed a kiss to his shoulder blade.

He turned around and pulled her close again. Her chest rose and fell rapidly, and she didn't try to pull away from his obvious arousal. In fact, she slid her arms around his waist and pulled him close.

"We need to find a way out of here," he whispered.

Her breath caught. "No." She shook her head.

"Yes. We might be able to make it. He can't have enough men to guard every inch of this mountain."

"You don't know what he'll do to you if you try to escape."

He cradled the back of her head in his palm. "He's going to kill us if we stay here."

She stiffened and shook her head again. Her fists doubled against the small of his back. "Rook, he'll torture you and leave you to bleed to death on the ground."

"So I should just give up without a fight? Without trying?"

She brought her fists around and up to pound on his chest. "You—man!" she hissed. "Your reasoning makes no sense. It will be better, because he promised me. He will give us this night together. He will give you—" her breath caught in a sob "—a dignified execution by firing squad."

"And for you?"

She didn't answer.

"That's what I thought. What would you have me do?"

"Preferably? Rain the punishment of God down on his head. Kill him, no matter if we die with him. Rid the planet of his insane power."

Rook nodded. "That's the plan," he breathed in her ear. Then he tugged on her earlobe with his teeth and followed them with his tongue, tracing its delicate curves all the way around and back to the lobe, which he nibbled again.

Irina's entire body tingled with arousal as Rook teased her ear. He knew what he was doing. He could always get his way by nibbling on her earlobe.

Right now, his teasing added to her already turned-on state. Her body soared to the brink of climax.

The dire task of making sure Rook's torso hadn't been bugged had turned into an erotic interlude unlike anything she'd ever experienced. She had no way of measuring how long it had taken to search every inch of his upper body, but for her, time had stood still, as if she'd been trapped forever in an erotic time warp of foreplay. Every place she'd touched, every millimeter of his skin had hummed with warmth, with life, with sexual stimulation.

"Rina." His voice buzzed in her ear, like a bee.

He took her fist in his hand and uncurled it gently, then guided it to the ball of his shoulder. "Feel," he whispered.

She ran her palm and then her fingers over his smooth skin, his shoulder bone, his strong, tense tendons.

Then she felt it. The tiny hard circle, right behind the ball and socket of his right shoulder.

"What is that?" she whispered, her heart pounding at the possibility that formed in her mind.

"A GPS locator chip. Brand-new technology. But I need to get outside."

A tracking device. He'd done what Ordo had ordered him not to do, on pain of death—his *and* hers. He'd brought reinforcements.

She lifted her face until her lips were almost touching his.

"Blow out the candles."

"What?"

"I slept here last night. Trust me."

His brows rose, but he did what she'd said. As he extinguished the last candle, he realized there was still light coming from somewhere. He glanced around but didn't see any other flames.

While he'd been busy with the candles, she'd lain on the bed. He could see her skin, pale against the dark, rich colors of the spread and drapes.

"Come here," she said softly.

After an instant's hesitation, he climbed onto the bed and lay beside her.

"Look up," she whispered in his ear.

He did. Directly over the bed was an opening in the cave roof. Not a large one. Just enough to let moonlight in and to see a few stars.

Just enough to—

Rook's astonished gaze met hers. She nodded.

Then she saw something she'd only seen a few times since she'd known him, and not once since he'd come back from the dead.

His smile.

No diamond could match it for beauty, or rarity. It transformed his stern, angular face into dimpled, boyish, heartbreaking sweetness.

With a little luck, the skies would stay clear tonight, and Deke and whoever else Rook had brought with him could zero in on the chip embedded in his shoulder.

"You should stay on top," she said, her voice breaking with hope and happiness and fear.

"I suppose I should." He touched the hem of her *abaya,* and she raised up so he could slip it off.

Then he reached for a length of gauzy cloth and draped it over them from head to toe.

She slid her hand between the cloth and his shoulder and touched the chip. He lay his hand over hers. "Thin cloth—not a problem."

Then in one smooth motion, he raised himself above her, and the hairs on his chest tickled her breasts' distended tips. His hips met hers, and his erection pushed against her with exquisite pressure. He leaned on his elbows and caressed her face, her cheeks, her lips, with his fingers.

All she wanted to do was surround herself with him. To have him in her and around her for this one last time.

Maybe his plan would work. Maybe they'd be rescued in the morning. But she knew that all she could count on was right now. All anyone ever had was now.

As much as she'd ever wanted anything, she wanted to hold on to it, to experience every single nanosecond of it. For this one brief instant of time, she had her heart's desire.

But more than that, she longed to hear him say the words he'd never said.

She hated herself right now. She knew this moment was fleeting, and she knew she was going to ruin it. But her insecurities were stronger than her will.

"Rook?"

"Hmm?" He kissed her deeply, thoroughly, a kiss to transcend time and space. A kiss between lovers. Then he pushed into her waiting body with exquisite slowness.

The sensation of him filling her made her cry. She'd been alone for so long. She'd given up hope, and yet hope had never given up on her.

He made a noise deep in his throat and sank deeper. He pressed his forehead against hers. She felt his chest rise and fall rapidly.

"This feels so good," he whispered. "I missed you so much."

"Why, Rook?" she murmured brokenly. "Why did you leave me?"

"Rina," he muttered, his tone hovering between a warning and an endearment. Dipping his head, he sought her mouth.

She longed to kiss him, to surround herself with his powerful body, to feel him at once in her and around her as she had so many times before.

But inevitably, her hands pushed at his chest, resisting. She struggled to maintain eye contact.

"Why?" she repeated, like lines in a play she was being forced to perform. She wished she could stop, but she was too caught up in her nightmare.

"You know why," he whispered, and his breath fanned her eyelashes. He kissed her eyelids, her cheek, the sweet spot beneath her earlobe.

She tasted sweat on his neck—salty, delicious. "Rook, I need to know."

"I had to," he said. "It was the only way to keep you safe." His erection pulsed inside her.

"But you left me alone."

"Don't," he whispered, moving within her, rocking her with the slow rhythm she knew so well. His chest rumbled with languid laughter when she gasped.

But then she pushed him away again, helpless against the current of her insecurity and need.

He stopped again. "Rina, I know you don't trust me. I know I destroyed that when I did what I did. But you have to try. You have to believe me. I did it because I love you. So much that I believed that nothing, not even death, could tear us apart. I loved you then. I love you now. I will love you forever, wherever we are."

He held her gaze and pushed into her, once, twice, again and again, stealing the doubt from her mind and replacing it with uncontrollable desire.

"Now shut up and come with me." He pushed her over the threshold, and all the stars in the heavens burst in front of her eyes.

THE NEXT THING Irina knew, a man was poking a rifle into her neck. Her eyes flew open and her hand clutched at the thin cloth that covered her.

Rook was already awake and sitting up, his hands spread in a gesture of surrender. He spoke sharply, in the language of the area, and jerked his head toward the cloth-draped doorway that divided the bedroom from the main cave.

The rifle at her throat jabbed, choking her. She coughed.

The other soldier barked a command, and her guard took a step away. Then the two of them backed out of the room.

Rook's gaze met hers. "Are you okay?"

"What did you say to them?"

"Told them you were a lady and needed your privacy to dress."

She looked around and then up, at the opening in the roof. "It is barely dawn." Her heart leapt into her throat. "Is it time?"

He nodded grimly. "Apparently."

Rising, he walked naked around the bed and picked up the carafe of water. He poured a cup, handed it to her and turned the carafe up to his lips.

She drank some of the flat-tasting water, but it was hard to force it past the lump in her throat.

This was it. They were going to die today. A flood of regret washed over her. She wasn't old. Not even thirty-one.

There had been times in her life when she'd almost wanted to die. *Almost.* But today wasn't one of them.

Rook bent and picked up her *abaya* and tossed it to her. He looked her way but didn't meet her eyes. That could only mean one of two things—he was hiding something from her, or he'd lied to her.

She longed to ask him if they were really going to die here. To ask him why Deke wasn't on his way to rescue them. And why he wasn't fighting to live. But she was afraid of his answer. She'd thought she knew him, sometimes better than she knew herself. But he'd planned to fake his death, and she'd never suspected.

She pulled the *abaya* on over her head and stood so the hem fell to her ankles.

Rook buttoned his wrinkled, dirt-stained shirt and pulled on his pants, then shot his cuffs as if he were wearing a tux.

"Rook?"

In the dimness, his eyes, which were usually the color of peridot, looked much darker. A ghost of a smile played around his lips. "Don't be afraid, Rina," he murmured.

Her heart leapt and her breath caught. Was that assurance she heard in his voice? Maybe Deke was on his way.

He put an arm around her shoulders and pressed a kiss to the top of her head. "It's not so bad."

Death.

He was talking about death. Her throat closed and her eyes stung. Because he knew. She slid her arms around his waist and pressed her face into the hollow of his shoulder.

It was too late.

"I cannot help it," she whispered brokenly. "I wanted more. More time, more life. More *you*."

"Shh. Don't cry."

She *was* crying and she hated that she was that weak. He'd been so strong through everything. He'd been her rock. Her savior. Her lover.

She heard heavy footsteps. The guards.

Rook gently pushed her away but kept his hand on the small of her back. The guards entered and stood on either side of the cave opening, their rifles cradled menacingly in their arms.

Pressing firmly on her back, Rook urged her forward. She lifted her head, doubled her fists at her sides and walked through the opening with as much dignity as she could gather.

In the large main cave, Novus Ordo sat with a cup in his hand. "Coffee?" he said conversationally. "It's strong."

Rook pulled her a few millimeters closer. He didn't answer the terrorist.

"No?" Ordo drained the cup and held it out. The old woman standing behind him took it. "See that?" he asked with a grin. "There's nothing like it. Think I could ever have all this in the U.S.?"

"And I thought you were crazy and misguided, but at least you had a worthy cause." Rook's voice dripped with revulsion. "Looks like your thing isn't saving the planet—it's power and money."

Ordo's face turned dark. "Don't even presume to judge me," he shouted, his hands white-knuckled on the arms of his chair. But immediately, he let go and held up his hands, palms out.

"No," he said, shaking his head. "I'm not going to let you bait me this morning. I intend to enjoy this."

He turned to Irina. "Mrs. Castle, you kept your word. I'm going to keep mine. Your husband will be executed by a firing squad this morning."

Irina couldn't speak. She could hardly breathe. To hear those words, spoken in that calm, slightly amused voice chilled her to her soul.

"What about my wife?" Rook asked. "You'll let her go?"

Ordo laughed. "Sure. Sure thing. I'll let her go." He said something else, in that language Irina couldn't understand, and all the soldiers in the room laughed, too.

Rook's whole body went rigid against her, and she felt his hand double into a fist at her back.

What had Ordo said? She looked fearfully at the terrorist and the two guards standing on either side of him. They were leering at her. Her knees gave way, and she'd have fallen if Rook hadn't caught her.

"Kill me," she whispered to him as he held her close against him.

He didn't answer her, but his arms tightened and his heartbeat against her ear tripled.

"Mrs. Castle. I'm guessing you figured out what I said." Ordo grinned at her. "And, no, your husband won't be able to kill you. He doesn't have the means or the guts, do you, Colonel—?"

The last of his sentence was drowned out by the sound of an airplane overhead.

Ordo's head jerked up sharply, then he eyed Rook with suspicion. He gestured to one of his guards and whispered in his ear. The guard nodded. He stepped away from Ordo's chair and headed for the main entrance to the cave, taking another soldier with him.

Novus Ordo slammed his fist on the chair arm. "I *knew* it. You couldn't keep your word, could you?" he thundered. "You coward! You cheat! Well, I hope that's your best buddy up there in that plane, because it's coming *down!*"

He pointed to one of his guards and spat an order, then pointed to a second one. The two men slung their rifles over their shoulders. One grabbed Rook, the other grabbed her.

He was separating them. Irina struggled helplessly against the guard holding her, as she tried to maintain eye contact with Rook.

He hadn't reacted to the guard who'd dragged him across the room. He stood tall and straight, and when his gaze met hers, he gave her a tiny shake of his head.

Don't struggle. It was as clear as if he'd said it aloud.

From outside, she heard several small explosions, one right after another. She sent a questioning glance toward Rook but he was looking at Novus, who held his hand up.

He waited. The whole room waited.

Another short burst of explosive, then a deafening blast that went on for a couple of seconds.

No one in the room moved.

Finally, the unmistakable sound of metal crashing to the ground.

Irina gasped. Rook closed his eyes. Novus Ordo

sent up a shout of triumph, and the roomful of guards cheered with him.

There could be only one explanation for what she'd heard.

Novus had shot down their rescue plane.

Chapter Fourteen

Rook looked Novus Ordo in the eye and watched him light up like a child on Christmas as the sickening sound of metal crashing to the ground filled the air.

Novus smirked at him in triumph. "Did you think I wouldn't have anti-aircraft missiles? Did you think I couldn't shoot your little planes right out of the air?"

Rook let the words roll off him like beads of water. He didn't change expression, didn't move a muscle. The hardest thing was not to look at Rina, but he managed. He held Ordo's gaze.

After a beat, Novus snapped an order and all the guards stood at attention. Best Rook could translate was something on the order of "It's time. Make ready."

He figured Novus was ordering his men to set up the firing squad. A shard of fear ripped through Rook. He hoped his courage held out. He wasn't sure how much he had left. It had been draining away ever since the moment he found out Novus had gotten his hands on Irina. And now, if he died, or maybe even if he managed to get out of this alive, his sister was a target.

As he expected, a second guard stepped up beside

him. From the corner of his eye he saw one move to Irina's right.

With a rifle barrel pressed into his kidney, he was marched through the tent and outside. The bright sunlight was obscured by black smoke. To his left, a coil of fire and smoke rose several hundred feet into the air.

The planes. He turned his attention to the guard in front of him, who gestured toward the south corner of the small open area. The guard behind him prodded him until he reached the edge of a stand of scrubby trees.

The guard drew a line with the toe of one boot, then pointed his rifle barrel at it. Rook stepped to the line and turned around.

The first thing he saw was Irina's pale face as she was prodded through the tent opening behind Novus Ordo. Her blue eyes were wide and dark with fear. When she spotted him, she swayed and caught at Ordo's shirt. He slung her off with a growl.

Immediately two guards grabbed her and pulled her away from their leader. One jerked her backward and shoved her toward an older woman, who grabbed her arm.

At least she was no longer beside Ordo.

Rook caught her gaze, wishing he could send her a telepathic message to reassure her. But if she could read his mind, she'd know how little reassurance he had to offer.

Then a small commotion to his left caught his attention. A man with a cloth over his head, hobbles on his feet and his hands tied behind his back was thrust into the clearing. He fell without even trying to right himself.

Ordo smiled at Rook. "That's right, Colonel." He

walked over to where the man was lying on the ground, pulled the cloth off the tethered man's head and lifted it by his hair.

It was Aaron Gold.

Rook frowned. Irina uttered a little cry.

Aaron's face was a mask of terror. A cut above his eye and a dark bruise on his cheek told Rook that Ordo hadn't welcomed him like a hero for betraying his boss and his country.

"So," Ordo said, turning to look at Rook. "Say hi to your employee of the month. I think he expected me to hand over the keys to the kingdom, or at least to a sizable reward." Ordo grinned at Rook. "Tell him why he's here."

Rook didn't speak.

"Tell him!"

Rook gritted his teeth. He didn't know how far he could push Ordo, so he answered, never taking his eyes off him. "Not even a traitor can trust a traitor."

Ordo laughed out loud. "That's right." He gestured to the guard, who yanked Aaron up and half dragged him over beside Rook.

"Tell him how lucky he is to be executed nobly, along with you."

Rook kept his mouth shut. Beside him, Aaron whimpered.

"Never mind." Novus Ordo waved a hand. "He knows. Since he's been here he's seen an example or two." He looked up at the morning sky. "Okay, let's get this show on the road. I've got a shipment of weapons coming into port in forty-eight hours. So I've got a long drive and a long flight ahead of me."

He gave an order, and ten soldiers stepped forward from various places in the clearing. They took their positions in an invisible line about twenty feet in front of Rook.

Rook lifted his head and tensed his muscles. He couldn't resist one last glimpse of Rina. When their gazes met, his heart leapt into his throat and tears burned at the backs of his eyes.

"Ready…" Ordo shouted.

Rook nodded at Rina. "Close your eyes," he whispered, but she didn't react. Of course she didn't. She couldn't hear him.

"Aim…"

Irina couldn't tear her gaze away from Rook's. He'd mouthed *Close your eyes,* but she couldn't. Wouldn't. She tried to jerk away from the old woman, to run to him and die beside him, but the woman's grip was too strong.

She waited, cringing, determined to stand strong for Rook, as Novus Ordo uttered the final word—

"Fire."

Something popped.

Rook's head jerked. Aaron screamed.

Ordo made a strangled noise, then collapsed, not two feet in front of her.

Then everyone was shouting. Gunfire burst all around her. Irina felt as if every single bullet hit her heart. Suddenly the black smoke from the downed planes swirled with white smoke from the guns and she couldn't see anything.

The old woman pulled on her sleeve, trying to force her to the ground out of the line of fire, but she had to find Rook.

The woman let go, and Irina fell to her knees, just as something hit her and knocked her backward.

"Stay down!" The command was growled and

constant gunfire obscured the words, but she knew who it was.

"Rook! Thank God!"

He slid his arm underneath hers and dragged her through the tent into the cave. "Stay!" He thrust a long rifle into her hands. "Shoot to kill. It'll keep firing as long as you hold the trigger down."

"Wait!" she shrieked, but he was already gone.

Back out there.

The guns still spat unrelenting staccato bursts. She knew the sound. From her childhood in Russia. Back then, she'd believed that her mother and father would keep her safe.

Now she knew better.

She scooted backward until the rocky cave wall stopped her. She quickly examined the heavy rifle. She'd never seen one like it, but it seemed to have all the necessary parts.

Did it matter that she'd never shot a gun like this in her life?

Hold the trigger down—it keeps shooting.

She planned to do exactly that.

ROOK CROUCHED behind the dead body of an enemy soldier and swung the barrel of his weapon around, squinting to see through the smoke. The ground was littered with bodies. He prayed none of them were his men.

He knew going in that his rescue squad would be grossly outnumbered, but it looked as if he'd been right in his assessment of the situation.

Most of Novus Ordo's rag-tag band of soldiers had scattered at the sight of Ordo with a bullet hole in the middle of his forehead. They'd probably fled to higher and more remote caves. Obviously, they were braver carrying a suicide bomb than fighting hand-to-hand.

Ordo's fatal mistake was that he hadn't recruited soldiers—he'd recruited zealots.

Rook scooted backward awkwardly, still eyeing the carnage, alert in case one of the sprawled bodies moved or another soldier came into sight.

Finally he reached the opening. With difficulty, he pushed himself up to a crouched position and cautiously stepped inside. Empty.

He ran his hand down his right pant leg, feeling the blood that soaked it. Gingerly touching the painful wound, he decided it had stopped bleeding, which was a relief.

He limped across the stone floor, planted his back against the wall and angled around, leading with the automatic rifle he'd taken off one of the casualties.

The cave was dark, the air inside it still. It felt and sounded empty. Without breathing, he turned toward the corner where he'd left Irina.

"Stop!" she cried.

He froze. "Rina? It's me."

For an instant he heard nothing. Then a small sound, like a sob. "Is it over?"

"I think so." He braced himself on his good leg and waited for her to throw herself into his arms. Once he felt her body, vibrant and warm against him, then he'd know for sure it was over. That they had survived. *Then,* he could reassure her.

But she didn't run to him. He could see her, pale skin lighter than the shadows. She stood slowly and walked carefully toward him, cradling the rifle like an expert.

"Rina, are you all right?"

Without speaking, she stepped into the thin blade of

light that shone from the cave opening. Her wide, blue eyes assessed him from head to toe. When they reached his legs, she gasped audibly, then raised her gaze to his.

"Who died in the planes?"

He gave her a small smile. "No one. They were drones. Piloted by remote control. I didn't see any Americans on the ground, either, so I'm hoping we haven't lost anyone. Most of Ordo's men have scattered. We'll never see them again. Brock and Deke should be here any time."

"You lied to me," she stated calmly.

"No, Rina—" He held out a hand, but she ignored it.

"Yes, you did." She lifted the heavy rifle to her shoulder, aimed the barrel at his eye and lay her cheek along the stock.

He didn't move. If she shot him, he couldn't blame her. But it wasn't her style. She wasn't vengeful.

After a few seconds she lowered it again. "How many times do you expect me to watch you die?"

"Rina, you have to understand—"

"I do not *have* to do anything except endure until I can get home."

He heard footsteps outside the cave. He turned, raising the rifle.

"Rook? Irina?" The voice was unmistakable.

"Deke," he said on a relieved sigh. "In here," he called.

Deke strode into the cave, dressed in desert camo with matching paint on his face. His dark eyes took in the tense scene immediately. "Everything okay?"

Rook nodded. "Anybody hurt?"

Deke shook his head. "A couple of guys got winged, but this new body armor is amazing." He nodded at

Rook's leg with a frown. "I see you weren't quite so lucky. We need to get that looked at."

He glanced at Irina. "Irina? You're all right?" he asked gently.

"I'm fine." Her voice cut the air like a bayonet.

Deke's head shot up a fraction. "O-kay. Good. Let's get you two out of here and into one of the choppers."

As if conjured by Deke's words, the slap of helicopter blades hit Rook's ears.

Irina heard them, too. She carefully set the rifle down on the floor of the cave and then addressed Deke.

"Is it safe to go out there now?"

"Yes, ma'am," Deke replied. "Brock's waiting right outside the tent."

She turned and stalked out.

Rook waited, his mouth compressed into a thin line. Sure enough, as soon as she disappeared, Deke turned on him.

"I told you to tell her."

"You're out of line," Rook said evenly. "You do *not* know my wife better than I do."

"Oh, yeah? You still think she's the innocent young daughter of Leonid Tankien that you brought out of the former Soviet Union. You still think she needs to be sheltered. But you're wrong. That's not who she is."

Rook eyed his best friend and oath brother. Something scary filled his insides. Something he'd felt only a couple of times in his life.

Self-doubt.

Deke stuck his finger in front of Rook's face. "See. You *know* I'm right. Hah. You've dug a deep hole for yourself this time, Castle. I told you not to hurt her. I hope you can dig yourself out. Now, let's get that leg bandaged—" Deke paused, enjoying himself way too much "—unless you're going to heal it with stubbornness."

Rook pushed past his best friend and strode out of the cave, mustering as much dignity as he could. He'd have done a better job of it if his damn leg hadn't been hurting so much.

Chapter Fifteen

Rook looked around the conference room at his two oath brothers. They were a little worse for wear, but they were alive.

"There was a time there when I wasn't sure we were going to make it"

Matt nodded.

Deke leaned back in his chair.

"As soon as we get back from Washington, I want each of you to take your families on a long honeymoon. You've earned it. You deserve it."

"Yeah?" Deke responded. "What about you?"

Rook looked over Deke's shoulder at the big picture window. He rubbed his chin. "I've got a couple of things I need to take care of."

"You need to take care of? What about Irina? If you want my opinion—"

He glared at his best friend. "I don't."

"Maybe not. But you need it," Deke continued. "Matt, help me out here."

Rook turned toward Matt, daring him to speak.

Matt didn't look away, but he didn't speak, either.

"Tell him, Matt. Tell him what an idiot he is, hanging on to his pride. How being too damn stubborn to admit he's wrong could lose him the best thing that ever happened to him."

Rook and Matt both turned toward their friend, whose face turned red. "Hey. It's just my opinion."

Rook shook his head. "I can't fix this. I hurt her too much. Betrayed her too many times. She'll never trust me."

Deke growled. "You don't give her enough credit. You never have."

Matt pushed back from the table. "We've only got about twenty minutes before the limos get here to take us to the airport.

"I've got to make sure Aimee and William are ready."

"Yeah," Deke responded. "I need to say goodbye to Mindy. She's not happy that the doctor won't let her fly."

"Why don't you stay with her?"

"I would if she let me. But she's threatened me with bodily harm if I don't go to D.C. to meet the president."

Rook nodded. "Thanks, guys. See you on the plane."

SHE DIDN'T LOOK ANY DIFFERENT.

Irina stared at her reflection in the mirror, disbelieving. She turned sideways. The simple teal-blue jersey dress hugged her curves exactly the same way it always had. Her silhouette wasn't any leaner—or curvier.

She leaned in closer, inspecting her face. No new wrinkles or gray hairs.

Of course it had only been three weeks since she'd

found out her dead husband wasn't dead. Twenty days. She shook her head. It felt like twenty years.

The tears started again. She hadn't been able to control them since she'd started the seemingly endless journey from Mahjidastan back to Wyoming.

She'd never cried so much in her life. Crying never helped anything, and it could be dangerous. She'd learned that during her childhood in Russia. Her mother, and later her father, had warned her countless times that if she cried, the soldiers would find them.

She yanked another tissue from the box and dabbed at her eyes, lecturing herself silently.

She heard a knock on the door to her suite.

"Come in," she called, working to keep her voice steady. "My bags are ready to go."

She quickly gathered up all the wadded tissue, cardboard packaging and other rubbish from the countertop and tossed it into the trash, looked at herself one more time and stepped out of the dressing room.

And stopped dead still.

It wasn't the limo driver come to pick up her bags.

It was Rook. He was as handsome as ever in crisply pressed khakis and a green crewneck sweater that matched his eyes. The slight bulge of the bandage on his thigh was hardly noticeable.

She pressed her lips together and braced herself to meet his gaze. He was watching her warily, unsure of what she was going to do or say.

Good. He deserved to experience the fear and uncertainty she'd lived with for the past two years.

"You look beautiful—"

"Don't," she snapped.

His jaw tensed. "The limo will be here in a half hour."

Smoothing her dress over her ribs and tummy with her palms, she took a deep breath and nodded. "I'm ready. Thank you."

He didn't move.

"There is no need for you to wait. I will be out in a few minutes. I just want to—"

"Rina, you've been crying."

"No, I haven't."

Did he have to be so observant? So gentle? She hated the way he was acting—had acted ever since they got back—as if she were fine porcelain and he was terrified she might break.

Where was the arrogant commander who took charge and damn the consequences?

"We need to talk. You haven't said two words to me since we got back. It's been eight days."

Her stupid tears were clogging her throat again. She swallowed hard. "Please go. I'll be right out there—"

"No," he barked.

Great. *Now* he pulled out his commander ammo.

She turned her back on him. "Go," she choked. "I will get my purse."

"I'm not leaving."

He'd come closer. Too close. He put his hand on her arm. Any second now she was going to break down in front of him. And he'd be proven right. She was weak. She did need his protection.

She really couldn't live without him.

She had only one line of defense left. She hadn't wanted to tell him this so soon. She'd wanted to keep it a secret as long as she could, because it was the one weapon she knew would find its mark.

The one thing guaranteed to send him hightailing it away from her like a jackrabbit from a fox.

She whirled, her face only inches from his.

"I'm pregnant," she spat. For the moment, abject terror and heavy dread dried up her tears.

He'd never wanted children. She'd always known that.

Early on, he'd listened when she brought it up. He'd never commented, but he had listened. In the months leading up to his death—his disappearance, rather—he'd refused to even talk about the possibility.

Now, standing so close to him she could feel his heat, she watched in fearful fascination as her words sank in.

His head moved almost imperceptibly, as if he were dodging a glancing blow. Then his brow wrinkled and his eyes glittered with something she couldn't identify.

"You're pregnant? How?" he shook his head.

She swallowed a giggle that could have just as easily been a sob. "How do you think?"

He shook his head slowly, dazedly. "I don't know," he muttered. "I never thought—"

He dropped his gaze to his boots and rubbed his palm across his mouth, then shook his head again. "I never—"

Rook Castle, speechless? She wasn't sure what she'd expected. Anger? Indifference? But not this uncertainty.

The adrenaline rush of fear and dread was fading and the tears were pushing their way to the surface again. She felt one slip over her lower lid and tickle its way down her cheek.

Dammit. She swiped at it.

Rook pressed his knuckles against his lips, then looked up at her from under his lashes. After a second, his gaze drifted downward to her tummy and back up.

"You're really—?"

She nodded, dislodging another tear. "I'm sorry. I

know you never did want children. I understand why. I do. It was wonderful of you to marry me. You felt responsible, and I will always appreciate that."

While she was babbling, Rook's head shot up and his brows drew down in a frown.

"Rina, what the hell are you talking about?"

His eyes were glittering strangely, and his dark, thick lashes were matted, almost as if—as if they were wet.

"I—don't know," she answered.

"I've lived my life on the edge. I never thought it would be fair to a child. Especially after I saw every day what living that way had done—was doing—to you."

"Why did you marry me?"

A knock on the door interrupted his answer.

Annoyance briefly marred his features. "In a minute," he called.

"Rina—" His tone was something between a warning and an endearment, and there she was, back in the nightmare.

Her heart stood still.

"Colonel Castle?" a deferential voice called. "The limo is here."

"Tell them to wait!"

He put his hands on either side of her head and wiped her tears away with a gentle brush of his thumbs. Then he pressed his forehead to hers.

"You know why I married you," he whispered, his breath tickling her eyelashes.

"I don't," she said, caught in her recurring dream, dreading the words she knew she was destined to say. Dreading the answer she already knew he would give.

"Tell me," she begged. It was happening just like in her dream. Oh, she was pathetic.

He sighed, then lifted his head. A jagged shadow defined the clean line of his jaw.

"I had to marry you," he said. "I thought it was the only way I could protect you."

"But what about love?" *Stop! Don't say it.* But it was too late.

"Love? Rina—" His voice rasped. "Don't you remember what I said that night in the cave?"

Her broken heart ached. Of course she did. Every word was tucked away in the farthest corner of her heart. She would remember and cherish those words forever. That didn't mean she believed them.

"You didn't believe me." An echo of her thought.

He kissed her forehead and then straightened. "I don't know how to fix this. I made a cocky, arrogant assumption, that just because I loved you, I could keep you safe."

He sighed. "I'll do whatever you want. I'll let you go, I'll stay away from my—" his voice broke harshly "—my child. But whatever you decide to do, please try to believe me. I do love you. I loved you the first moment I laid eyes on you. And I'll love you forever."

Irina could barely breathe around the squeezing of her heart. She'd wanted desperately to believe those words he'd said that night in Novus Ordo's cave. And she desperately wanted to believe him now.

But he wasn't meeting her gaze. And she knew from long experience that it meant he was holding something back. She touched his chin.

"Look at me," she said as evenly as she could. His olive-green eyes met hers. In their depths, she saw why he'd avoided her gaze. Not because he was hiding a secret.

Not this time.

What she saw was doubt—self-doubt. That was

what he was trying to hide. The fact that he was doubting himself pierced her heart like an arrow.

"No," she murmured.

Pain flickered across his features.

"No. My husband will not stay away from his child. Not for one moment—until at least she is twenty-one."

She'd read in books about people's faces lighting up, but she'd never witnessed it in real life—until this moment. Rook's face glowed with an angelic light.

"Rina?" he whispered, twirling her around and pulling her back against him. "I'm sorry—"

She put her fingers to his lips. "Shh. I accept your apology."

He kissed her shoulder, the side of her neck and her ear. Then he whispered, "You didn't let me finish."

His hands slid over her belly, where their tiny new baby lay, protected by her womb.

She laughed through tears. "Please then," she murmured, laying her head back against his shoulder and closing her eyes. "Finish."

"I'm sorry, but this—" he patted her tummy "—is not a girl. He's all boy."

Laughter bubbled up from her throat. Laughter, joy, love. She turned in his arms and lifted her face to his. "We'll see."

In one motion, Rook picked her up and headed toward the bed. But before he'd gotten two feet, a sharp pounding stopped him.

"Colonel Castle. Is everything all right? Because if we don't leave now, you're going to miss your plane to Washington. And that means you'll miss the ceremony with the president tomorrow morning."

With a growl, he set her back down.

"We're coming, right now," Irina called breathlessly.

Rook held on to her for one more second, long enough to whisper in her ear.

She laughed and shook her head. "You will do no such thing in the limo. And not on the plane, either. We have plenty of time."

Saying the words, she realized that, for the first time, she believed them.

"We have a lifetime," she whispered to herself, as her husband opened the door for her.

* * * * *

*Celebrate 60 years of pure reading pleasure
with Harlequin®!
Just in time for the holidays,
Silhouette Special Edition® is proud to present*
New York Times *bestselling author
Kathleen Eagle's
ONE COWBOY, ONE CHRISTMAS.*

Rodeo rider Zach Beaudry was a travelin' man—
until he broke down in middle-of-nowhere South
Dakota during a deep freeze. That's when an
angel came to his rescue....

"Don't die on me. Come on, Zel. You know how much I love you, girl. You're all I've got. Don't do this to me here. Not *now*."

But Zelda had quit on him, and Zach Beaudry had no one to blame but himself. He'd taken his sweet time hitting the road, and then miscalculated a shortcut. For all he knew he was a hundred miles from gas. But even if they were sitting next to a pump, the ten dollars he had in his pocket wouldn't get him out of South Dakota, which was not where he wanted to be right now. Not even his beloved pickup truck, Zelda, could get him much of anywhere on fumes. He was sitting out in the cold in the middle of nowhere. And getting colder.

He shifted the pickup into Neutral and pulled hard on the steering wheel, using the downhill slope to get her off the blacktop and into the roadside grass, where she shuddered to a standstill. He stroked the padded dash. "You'll be safe here."

But Zach would not. It was getting dark, and it was already too damn cold for his cowboy ass. Zach's battered body was a barometer, and he was feeling South

Dakota, big-time. He'd have given his right arm to be climbing into a hotel hot tub instead of a brutal blast of north wind. The right was his free arm anyway. Damn thing had lost altitude, touched some part of the bull and caused him a scoreless ride last time out.

It wasn't scoring him a ride this night, either. A carload of teenagers whizzed by, topping off the insult by laying on the horn as they passed him. It was at least twenty minutes before another vehicle came along. He stepped out and waved both arms this time, damn near getting himself killed. Whatever happened to *do unto others?* In places like this, decent people didn't leave each other stranded in the cold.

His face was feeling stiff, and he figured he'd better start walking before his toes went numb. He struck out for a distant yard light, the only sign of human habitation in sight. He couldn't tell how distant, but he knew he'd be hurting by the time he got there, and he was counting on some kindly old man to be answering the door. No shame among the lame.

It wasn't like Zach was fresh off the operating table—it had been a few months since his last round of repairs—but he hadn't given himself enough time. He'd lopped a couple of weeks off the near end of the doc's estimated recovery time, rigged up a brace, done some heavy-duty taping and climbed onto another bull. Hung in there for five seconds—four seconds past feeling the pop in his hip and three seconds short of the buzzer.

He could still feel the pain shooting down his leg with every step. Only this time he had to pick the damn thing up, swing it forward and drop it down again on his own.

Pride be damned, he just hoped *somebody* would be answering the door at the end of the road. The light in the front window was a good sign.

The four steps to the covered porch might as well have been four hundred, and he was looking to climb them with a lead weight chained to his left leg. His eyes were just as screwed up as his hip. Big black spots danced around with tiny red flashers, and he couldn't tell what was real and what wasn't. He stumbled over some shrubbery, steadied himself on the porch railing and peered between vertical slats.

There in the front window stood a spruce tree with a silver star affixed to the top. Zach was pretty sure the red sparks were all in his head, but the white lights twinkling by the hundreds throughout the huge tree, those were real. He wasn't too sure about the woman hanging the shiny balls. Most of her hair was caught up on her head and fastened in a curly clump, but the light captured by the escaped bits crowned her with a golden halo. Her face was a soft shadow, her body a willowy silhouette beneath a long white gown. If this was where the mind ran off to when cold started shutting down the rest of the body, then Zach's final worldly thought was, *This ain't such a bad way to go.*

If she would just turn to the window, he could die looking into the eyes of a Christmas angel.

* * * * *

Could this woman from Zach's past
get the lonesome cowboy to come in
from the cold...for good?
Look for
ONE COWBOY, ONE CHRISTMAS
by Kathleen Eagle.
Available December 2009
from Silhouette Special Edition®.

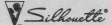

Silhouette *Desire*

New York Times Bestselling Author

SUSAN MALLERY

HIGH-POWERED, HOT-BLOODED

Innocently caught up in a corporate scandal, schoolteacher
Annie McCoy has no choice but to take the tempting deal offered
by ruthless CEO Duncan Patrick. Six passionate months later,
Annie realizes Duncan will move on, with or without her. Now
all she has to do is convince him she is the one he really wants!

Available December 2009 wherever you buy books.

ALWAYS POWERFUL, PASSIONATE AND PROVOCATIVE

Visit Silhouette Books at www.eHarlequin.com

™ *Silhouette*®

SPECIAL EDITION

**FROM *NEW YORK TIMES* AND *USA TODAY*
BESTSELLING AUTHOR**

KATHLEEN EAGLE

ONE COWBOY,
One Christmas

When bull rider Zach Beaudry appeared
out of thin air on Ann Drexler's ranch,
she thought she was seeing a ghost of
Christmas past. And though Zach had
no memory of their night of passion years
ago, they were about to share a future
he would never forget.

*Available December 2009
wherever books are sold.*

Visit Silhouette Books at www.eHarlequin.com

SSE65493

REQUEST YOUR FREE BOOKS!

2 FREE NOVELS PLUS 2 FREE GIFTS!

✦ HARLEQUIN®
INTRIGUE®

Breathtaking Romantic Suspense

YES! Please send me 2 FREE Harlequin Intrigue® novels and my 2 FREE gifts (gifts are worth about $10). After receiving them, if I don't wish to receive any more books, I can return the shipping statement marked "cancel." If I don't cancel, I will receive 6 brand-new novels every month and be billed just $4.24 per book in the U.S. or $4.99 per book in Canada. That's a savings of close to 15% off the cover price! It's quite a bargain! Shipping and handling is just 50¢ per book.* I understand that accepting the 2 free books and gifts places me under no obligation to buy anything. I can always return a shipment and cancel at any time. Even if I never buy another book from Harlequin, the two free books and gifts are mine to keep forever.

182 HDN EYTR   382 HDN EYT3

Name	(PLEASE PRINT)

Address	Apt. #

City	State/Prov.	Zip/Postal Code

Signature (if under 18, a parent or guardian must sign)

Mail to the **Harlequin Reader Service:**
IN U.S.A.: P.O. Box 1867, Buffalo, NY 14240-1867
IN CANADA: P.O. Box 609, Fort Erie, Ontario L2A 5X3

Not valid to current subscribers of Harlequin Intrigue books.

**Are you a current subscriber of Harlequin Intrigue books
and want to receive the larger-print edition?
Call 1-800-873-8635 today!**

* Terms and prices subject to change without notice. Prices do not include applicable taxes. Sales tax applicable in N.Y. Canadian residents will be charged applicable provincial taxes and GST. Offer not valid in Quebec. This offer is limited to one order per household. All orders subject to approval. Credit or debit balances in a customer's account(s) may be offset by any other outstanding balance owed by or to the customer. Please allow 4 to 6 weeks for delivery. Offer available while quantities last.

Your Privacy: Harlequin is committed to protecting your privacy. Our Privacy Policy is available online at www.eHarlequin.com or upon request from the Reader Service. From time to time we make our lists of customers available to reputable third parties who may have a product or service of interest to you. If you would prefer we not share your name and address, please check here. ☐

HI09R

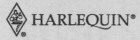

HARLEQUIN®

American ★ Romance®

A Cowboy Christmas
MARIN THOMAS

2 stories in 1!

The holidays are a rough time for widower
Logan Taylor and single dad Fletcher McFadden—
neither hunky cowboy has been lucky in love.
But Christmas is the season of miracles! Logan
meets his match in "A Christmas Baby," while
Fletcher gets a second chance at love in "Marry
Me, Cowboy." This year both cowboys are on
Santa's Nice list!

Available December
wherever books are sold.

"LOVE, HOME & HAPPINESS"

www.eHarlequin.com

HAR75292

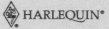
HARLEQUIN®

INTRIGUE®

COMING NEXT MONTH

Available December 8, 2009

#1173 FIRST NIGHT by Debra Webb
Colby Agency
To prove his innocence, a talented artist caught up in a murder investigation is in a race against time to catch the true killer—with the help of a Colby agent. And if they can survive the first night, their growing attraction may have a chance as well.

#1174 HIS SECRET CHRISTMAS BABY by Rita Herron
Guardian Angel Investigations
He returns to his hometown determined to forget the past, but a missing child—and the child's adoptive mother—calls out the P.I.'s protective instincts. Can he save the family he never dreamed he'd have?

#1175 SCENE OF THE CRIME: BRIDGEWATER, TEXAS
by Carla Cassidy
The small-town Texas sheriff has enough on his hands with a killer on the loose, but the feisty FBI profiler who insists on being a part of the case—against his wishes—may just be the woman he needs....

#1176 BEAUTY AND THE BADGE by Julie Miller
The Precinct: Brotherhood of the Badge
When the girl next door blows the whistle on illegal activities at work, the only person she can turn to for protection is her gruff cop neighbor—a man who is ready, willing and able to be her true-blue hero.

#1177 SECLUDED WITH THE COWBOY by Cassie Miles
Christmas at the Carlisles'
After rescuing his wife from a kidnapper, the cowboy is determined to seal the rift between them and remind her of their love. But when she comes under threat again, his actions may speak louder than words as he fights to save what's his.

#1178 POLICE PROTECTOR by Dani Sinclair
When she discovers that her sister and her sister's children are missing, a career-minded businesswoman turns to a take-charge detective to find them—and as he takes on the dangerous case, he shows her that family is what matters most....

HICNMBPA1109